AF613236

Mother, Have A Safe Trip

Carl Abrahamsson

TRAPARTbooks

Mother, Have A Safe Trip

ISBN 978-91-986242-1-2

Trapart Books
P.O. Box 8105
SE-104 20 Stockholm
Sweden

www.trapart.net
info@trapart.net

www.carlabrahamsson.com
www.patreon.com/vanessa23carl

1

Mary Ritterstadt sat down on her bed and pulled an old cardboard box close to her. She raised her head and looked into the mirror on the wall.

"Mirror, mirror on the wall, who's the craziest of all?", she whispered slowly.

It used to make her smile, but not anymore. Mary could see her own reflection all too well, and she wasn't really happy about a lot. 60 years old, grey hair, cold blue eyes, frail, sad, frustrated, wrinkled, alone.

When her parents had died (a year earlier), she was left with clearing out her own space and clearing up theirs. Now, finally, she had. She had moved into their house just outside of New York City. Not with an overwhelming sense of joy but rather just because they had expected her to. They'd been nice to her. She knew that and she was always grateful and emotional when thinking about them.

In times of sadness, and this was certainly such a time, she brought out the box. Letters, photographs, small mementos of a life that had passed by far too quickly, all stashed inside. They always provided a kind of immediate emotional escapism that she needed from time to time. More often than not, she realized every time she hesitantly returned to the cardboard box.

After pouring the contents all over the bed, she started sorting, the way she had a million times before. She always returned to a ruled black notebook, in which she had tried, also a long time ago, to write down memories from her youth. She wanted to remember more than she actually did or could, and this book had been an attempt at pushing on in this highly frustrating process.

Mary looked at her own reflection again. She sighed heavily and then opened the journal of her memories:

"'Please allow me to introduce myself.' It was one of my favorite lines from one of my favorite Rolling Stones songs. How I used to love them. I used to be a big music fan, immersing myself in the era, living for and through music. In that sense I wasn't really different from a lot of teenagers in the late 60s. I was just an average girl drawn into a miasmic musical movement. Although I was born and raised in New York, my parents wouldn't even let me go up to Woodstock with my friends – who all went anyway. But as soon as I turned 18, late 1969, I moved into a place of my own and devoted myself to what was going on. There was a lot.

I often dreamt of being a bird. A "high-flying bird", just like the Byrds had sung. Being light, being weightless, sweeping over mountains and forests and villages and cities but always returning to nature, to my own nest high up in a tree somewhere. The perspective was staggering and I tried to daydream the very same things. Often, it worked but not always. It felt nice when it did.

I went to Nepal in the autumn of 1970 with my friend Magdalene Miller, nickname: "Sparkles". Mine was "Glitters". We were both lovingly naïve hippie chicks and very proud of it. Love could change the world back then (or so we believed) and we wanted to help out. We tried going to Afghanistan first but couldn't make it. It was much easier to get to Kathmandu, so we did.

There was nothing we didn't immediately love about Kathmandu and Nepal. It was just so exotic, so colorful. As this was also my very first trip abroad, the impressions were in many ways overwhelming. Sparkles and Glitters cruised the markets, ate cheap food, stayed in a crummy hotel on "Freak Street", made some day trips to Pokhara and other smaller towns, went up to trek in the mountains. We both said we'd never ever leave and we believed it.

Every night, there was incredible pot to smoke. Rooftop cafés with friendly Nepalese, Americans and Europeans, just really grooving together. We hung out and felt that life could be no better than this. Psychedelic music from the States and of the local variety filled the evening air around us and mixed with the sweet scents of incense and Cannabis. It really was like living in a pleasantly embracing dream.

After about a week in town, we heard that the Fateful Head were either there or coming soon. Not to actually play but to relax and have a good time. We wanted to meet them of course. We loved them. And, as if by divine providence, we accidentally met up with someone from their gang, and he invited us to a big party they were having in the garden of their hotel. We couldn't believe the good luck of it all.

What can I say? There was also a chemist there with them, and we learned he was wanted by the FBI back home. We soon realized why. He wasn't only wanted by the "feds" but also by the "heads": millions of kids worldwide. He was the world infamous LSD-wizard Mosely-Manly and, of course, he was the center of the party's attention. We must have been some fifty people tripping for what felt like days, nights, weeks, aeons. I still can't describe it.

It was a defining moment – or possibly several – of my life in so many ways. Not only for all the usual cross-dimensional reasons I enjoyed so much – I was by then no newcomer to lysergic acid – but also because I had a lot of sex. A lot. As had Sparkles. I think. My memories of what went on were slightly blurred and mixed with fantasies, hallucinations, the glamorous presence of the Head and the exotic environment in itself. To say that everything was one big colorful and cosmic orgasm would be a heavy understatement.

When I eventually came to, me and Sparkles realized that we had probably been tripping for two or three days, at least. Although absolutely exhausted, we were filled with bliss and many insights. We must have scribbled a couple of notebooks each, with fragments, drawings, memories and descriptions. Where are those books now, I wonder?

We calmed down, gradually. At least Sparkles did. I seemed to linger on in a pleasant post-psychedelic state of mind. The colors were still more vivid. My mind was still buzzing. I didn't mind it. Not at all.

The band moved on soon after this and we didn't really care. We had had a great time with them, but we also needed to relax and see more of Kathmandu. We visited temples, ate, slept, listened to music, read books and just enjoyed our carefree life. Time passed without our noticing it. We were young, we had money and we did send off the occasional postcard to our moms and dads, always displaying a photo of a group of smiling, healthy Westerners trekking in the mountains.

One day, at the big Bodhnath stupa, we were having coffee and just watching the people swirl by. Some kind of old Baba man approached our table slowly and just looked at me. We thought that maybe we should give him some money, but he refused it and just smiled at me. At first it was charming, but after a couple of minutes we asked what he actually wanted.

"You have come here", he said.

We looked at each other and laughed.

"That's right, I have come here", I giggled.

"You're the mother", he continued.

"No, not really. I just glitter."

Me and Sparkles laughed again.

"You're the mother. This is fantastic."

"No, I'm not the mother."

"Yes, you're the mother."

"No, I am not the mother."

"Yes, you are very much the mother."

"Come on, Sparks, let's go", I said.

The Baba man was annoying me with his insisting. We paid and left. He just remained there, still smiling and waving at us.

"What was that all about?", Sparkles asked me as we left the Bodhnath area.

"You tell me. He was freaking me out, that's what."

"Let it go, Mary. Go with the flow. This is Kathmandu. Anything can happen, right?"

During the coming days, we both saw the Baba again. Always at a distance. He was completely harmless and always smiling, dressed in some kind of robe and with a long, grey beard. We couldn't really go to the police. He never really came close by either. We decided he just liked to watch bra-less blonde hippie chicks and after a while, that was OK with us too.

Then something happened. Or, rather, didn't happen. Sparkles stayed in bed one day, tired from having her period. I walked on my own around the Thamel neighborhood and, sure enough, the Baba man was close by too. It suddenly dawned upon me that I was overdue. I was usually a very regular woman, with cramps on clockwork. It had been more than a month since my last period and a mere three weeks since our acid orgy. I was struck with panic. What if…?

I couldn't speculate. A couple of days later I got an appointment at a Western-style clinic and more or less immediately got the reply I didn't want: I was 100% pregnant. Funnily enough, I couldn't see the Baba man around as I slowly walked back to Freak Street. I told Sparkles and we both cried and laughed and hugged each other. She thought it was so great. I didn't fully agree. And I realized I'd probably have to have a word or two with the Baba man. Not to mention with my parents.

I became depressed rather than excited. Who was the father? I asked Sparkles not to say anything to anyone and I trusted her. No mention of this to mom or dad or... Anyone.

Sparkles was great in all of this. She was honest and said that she wanted to go back home. I didn't. She suggested I stay and offered to lend me more money if I needed it. Maybe I should get into Yoga, go on a retreat, stop smoking pot, just take a time-out and think. I thought this was an excellent idea and I really loved her for the support.

After she'd left, I took a solitary walk through the neighborhoods I'd grown to love so much. When I saw the Baba at a distance, looking at me, I didn't hesitate at all. I walked up to him. We greeted.

"You're the mother", he started all over again.

"You're right. How could you know?"

"I know. Friend left?"

I nodded. Nothing strange about this. He could have seen Sparkles load her stuff into the taxi.

"You alone is no good. Come into mountains, breathe, breathe, breathe... Strong baby. I come tomorrow to hotel and we go to mountains."

I said nothing. Just nodded and that was that. I had no fear of the guy whatsoever. This trip had started pretty crazily, so why not carry on and see?

The next morning I checked out and thanked the management for everything. Then I sat on the staircase and waited, thinking of what mom and dad would say. Oh boy, if they only knew!

I expected a small Indian car would arrive or maybe we'd walk to a local bus. But from out of nowhere an elegant, modern Mercedes appeared, all black and impressive-looking. Surely this was some kind of mistake?

Baba stepped out of the Mercedes, as did a blonde man in his late twenties with piercing blue eyes. They put my bags in the trunk.

"Very nice to meet you", said the man, with a distinct German accent. We shook hands and his grip was tight, almost too tight. He looked a little bit concerned.

"Thanks. My name is Mary Ritterstadt and I sparkle and I glitter," I said.

"I know," he replied. "I am Govinda Harrer."

"I'm Big Yoga Baba", the Baba man said and laughed.

That was that. Me and Baba sat in the back seat and Govinda drove us out of Kathmandu and far, far up into the mountains. The scenery was amazing. Dense forests, small villages, peasants working hard, kids waving at us, animals drifting. The Mercedes drove through a timeless scenery and I finally became so tired that I dozed off.

Baba shook me gently and I awoke. We were there. Where? I didn't really know. But there we were. I was greeted by some Nepalese families and Baba introduced me. I could see Westerners too in the distance, mostly young people. I looked around. It was a mix of a village and some kind of retreat place. People were doing Yoga together while others were sitting together, reading books. There was something very serene about the place.

Everyone was kind to me. I was shown to my own room and some young girls helped me unpack. They didn't know any English but wanted to feel my belly. They did, and giggled. How could they tell? Or maybe my pregnancy really was some kind of big deal here and everyone knew about it?

Harrer was gone, as was the Mercedes. Baba waved at me to come sit down by his side. A man my own age introduced himself as Rama, Baba's son. He spoke English quite well, and Baba did too when he had to.

"Why am I here?", I asked them.

"This will probably sound a little bit fantastic to you, Mary," Rama began. "But it's destiny. You believe in destiny, no? My father saw you at the Bodhnath and knew right away. How should I put it? You're the mother of someone quite extraordinary. Someone we care for."

"I don't get it. How can you know?", I replied.

"I think you've been here long enough to see there's a lot of magic here. Strange things happen and it's... What's the term? No big deal for us. For you maybe, but for us, no. We have been waiting for this child. We knew it was coming, you see."

Big Baba nodded. He handed me a cup of tea and some biscuits, and I accepted them, looking at these weird guys.

"So you're saying I'm the future mother of someone you know is coming? I'm sorry, but I don't get it."

"You are a Western girl, Mary", Rama continued. "You can be amazed, take some acid, listen to music, read poetry, see things, think of it as a party. But here, it's all for real. It goes on. It never ends. And now you are here and it's also for real."

"And it never ends?", I asked.

"You are free to do as you like, Mary. Always. But that doesn't change that we're expecting this child just as much as you are."

"I'm very tired," I lied to them.

"OK. Go and sleep a little. Then food, then we talk," Big Baba said.

During the evening we walked together around the area. Some fifty people were in the commune to practice Yoga and study. Everyone I met said Hello very reverently – perhaps my two crazies had told them about their ideas, and these mellow-brains believed in it? I didn't mind one little bit though. I was treated royally and when I went to sleep that night I did so exhausted by a mix of my own disbelief and serene happiness.

Waking up, I felt strong. It was probably the first time I felt really pregnant too. It felt good. Some of the confusion had left me. While having breakfast in the shadow of a huge old tree – "older than the one at Bodhgaya", Big Baba had told me – I weighed the options. I could go back to America, tell my parents, and raise the child as best I could. Perhaps even try to get in touch with the Fateful Head. Or I could go back and have an abortion, which would be terrible. I couldn't finish the thought even, as images of Big Baba and Rama's devotion to my future child seemed so sincere.

Or... I could stay here in this apparent paradise, write mom and dad for more money, saying I want to become a Yoga teacher or something. Would that be bad? Wouldn't it actually be great? I knew I could trust Sparkles. I'd write her too. She'd understand.

After breakfast, I had already made up my mind. When Rama approached me, I looked at him and said right out, "If you don't mind, I'd like to stay here and have the baby and not have to think about anything else, thank you very much."

Rama smiled and thanked me. It was to his liking. He turned around to Big Baba, who was watching us, and shouted something in Nepali. Suddenly everyone who could hear it started to applaud and cheer. It felt a bit awkward, but I was happy nonetheless. Sometimes it's better to make a decision, even if you don't know where it'll lead."

2

Mary put the book down. Why was this so painful to read? The decision had been made, it was of her own free will. She realized that this phase had been so blissful and that wasn't the problem at all. On the contrary. She remembered that writing this journal had become harder and harder the closer to her departure she got.

"Calm, quietude, stillness, harmony. I knew I was really blessed by being blessed by this compound of Yogis and students. I asked no questions and it didn't seem strange. I tried to hand over some money at times, but Baba and Rama wouldn't hear of it.

When I was in my seventh month of pregnancy, Baba started talking to me about the situation as such. They believed the child would be an important teacher to them, and also to more people around the world. I tried to remain sane about it. I grew to believe it. He also specifically told me that it was important that they could raise the child there and teach it certain basic things: meditation, magic, religion. I was so happy being there that I didn't question any of it.

My parents wrote often and said they missed me. I missed them too, of course. Lying about everything made me feel bad. Baba suggested I go back to the US after the baby had been born, to sort things out. Just for a short while, and then come back. I was too immersed in my then present state to allow myself to consider anything but just being there and being pregnant. Again, I felt blessed."

Mary flipped through the following pages, as she had many times before. Childbirth, love, amazement, a healthy blue-eyed boy, joy all over. Everyone at the compound helped out and lovingly took care of both mother and child.

At the same time, increasingly frequent passages about America, her parents and how to deal with reality. She hadn't seen them in over a year. They wrote about coming over, as they were worried about her. Would they accept the child? Or, perhaps even more important, her keeping it a secret?

Passages in the journal followed in a more and more jumbled way. Six months after the baby had been born: back to the US without the child, everything still a secret. A clash of cultures and mind-frames. Heavy depression, and eventually a mental breakdown. Although Mary was an adult woman, her parents just wouldn't let her go back. Being separated from her child became overwhelmingly painful but she still didn't say anything. There was something inside her that echoed Rama and Baba: the child must remain in Nepal. At times, she didn't know if everything had been a dream or some kind of prolonged acid trip. She didn't have the energy to get back to Nepal on her own. Her parents, not really understanding what was going on, blamed the hippies, drugs and Yoga and committed her to a "resting home", where she was suddenly given other kinds of drugs and actively discouraged from doing Yoga. It seemed she had given up, but couldn't herself understand why this was happening, why she couldn't just shake it off and go back.

She kept the journal hidden from the world. The last entry said that she'd be going away for a while, which she was: to the resting home. "I feel I need to look at things from another perspective, not my own." Then, nothing.

As always when Mary looked through the box, and especially when re-reading the journal, she felt drained of energy. The notion that she had wasted forty years of her life in an emotional vacuum was immensely painful. To long for a child she had never seen after its infancy pierced her heart with hot needles, over and over.

She stayed in that home for a year, diagnosed with "drug addiction". As there was money in the family, she was well taken care of. When treated as some kind of druggie, she just played along. Therapy, fresh air, training. And then, when declared "healthy" again, her parents signed her up for an upscale secretary school, which she attended in a state of continued depression. Then work at various companies, ending with a long time at a company handling patents. It was OK, she thought. Perhaps it was not OK, but it was still OK. She felt zombified and just played along. Memories of colorful Nepal faded into grey.

When she turned 60, she had no family and had never had any desire to create one either. Occasional men, but not on any emotional level whatsoever. She had money, and after her parents had died, she had some more money. She knew that she would sooner or later have to address the pain that had been with her all her life. If not, she might as well end everything right here and now.

Had the Nepalese villagers stolen her child and brainwashed her that everything was cool? During the past year, ever since her parents had died, something had become obvious to her. It was originally some kind of weird shame that had made her go back to America. As much as she had longed to go back to Nepal, her own emotional concoctions had pulled her back with the excuse of "it's better this way". Now that her parents were dead, she could actually formulate the thought without her own feelings short-circuiting her entire existence.

Mary decided, right there and then, to write a letter, just to see what, if anything, was going on with all her old friends. She had never promised to be in touch. She had never promised not to be in touch either. But she was, of this she was certain, slowly going crazy. She wanted to know what had happened to her son. She had a right to.

So she did it. Just sat down and wrote it. There was nothing about the group online – she tried all kinds of search words and alternatives. Maybe they had ceased to exist? Writing the letter filled her with a sense of exhilaration. Gradually, she thought to herself, she wrote a hole in her own psychic wrap, and she knew this would somehow be a life changer, for good or perhaps for worse. It didn't matter anymore.

Mary addressed the letter to "Big Yoga Baba c/o the Patanjali Neophile Yoga Village", and wrote the name of the small town which she remembered was close by. She felt a lot better after she'd sent it away. She had now done what she could.

About a week afterwards, she started having weird dreams in the middle of the night. Lucid dreams, filled with faces, bodies, memories in a palimpsest jumble. She hadn't been stoned in a long time, but this almost felt the same. It was certainly pleasant and the only thing that scared her was the intensity of the images. It felt like she was awake at the same time and actually saw and heard things rather than just dreaming them. It went on, night after night. She knew something was happening.

3

A little bit more than a week after dreaming those dreams, Mary received a letter from Nepal. She could hardly believe she held it in her hands. It had almost been too easy, she thought. She sat down on the living room couch and slowly, nervously opened it.

"Dear Mary,

Namaste from Nepal.

The reception of your letter was a great surprise and an auspicious sign for us all. First, some news. Big Baba passed on five years ago but he talked about you often, wondering what you were up to. The commune has grown and we still teach meditation and yoga, but with considerably more students from all over the world. They all venerate you and your son, as do we. I suspect you haven't been in touch with him. We haven't either, I'm afraid. We raised him as our own for 23 years and taught him our ways, as we had agreed on. He grew up to be a bright boy. We schooled him and his big interests turned out to be writing, music, photography and philosophy – not at all surprising.

He never wanted to be a leader, although we tried. As demands slowly grew (everybody here looked up to him, and still do, as a god-prince) he felt uneasy, just as we had predicted. At age 23, he insisted on having a passport and he did, quite surprisingly, manage to get a Nepalese one. Then he was gone. Just like that. Of course we knew this would happen sooner or later. Initially, some people from here followed him at a distance in Bangkok, but he noticed them, of course, and told them to stop – which they did, of course. They would have done anything for him.

He traveled, wrote, made music, even studied magic with an assortment of types, from Satanists like August LeMonde in America to Taoists in Korea and Aleister Crowley-type magicians in Europe. We were happy about this too. We wanted him to see the world and make more magic, but then to return to us and lead us on. Unfortunately, he hasn't. Yet, I should add.

I enclose here some lyric sheets he sent some years ago. He was in a music band and toured and played. I hope you like them. I don't know what to make of them, but maybe you do?

We would very much like to keep in touch with you, Mary. We're not in touch with your son anymore but would like to be. Anything you can do to help will be appreciated. He really should return soon, as should you, by the way. Time may be an illusion, but nonetheless it moves too quickly.

With love and blessings, Rama (the son of Big Baba. You remember how we made love in the mountains one time?)"

Mary gasped for air. In just a short time she had been informed about something she had deliberately kept in a suppressed vacuum of sorts for decades. She cried. She wanted to call him up, but there was no phone number or even an e-mail address, just a post office box in that small mountain village. If only she could scream so loudly that it would be heard all the way to Nepal! She found herself shaking nervously on the bed.

Mary then flipped through the additional pages. They were typewritten poems. She tried to dry her tears but they just kept coming.

"Stereoscopic survival

By Victor Ritterstadt

Searching for substance – Searching for essence
I never realized – I always realized
The end never comes – New beginnings appear
To those that wait – To the restless
For no reason – For no reason
Forgotten fancies – Remembering the substance
Spent on bleak views – Passed through me

Dreamt of dreams – Faced real life
Filled with shapes – Empty and void
Disturbed by forms – Just nothing
The many and the few – And nobody
Searching for substance – Finding forgotten fancies
Searching for essence – Finding nothing
The world is empty – I am filled
Waiting to be filled – Waiting to discharge
Filled with nothing – Leave something behind
More than everything – Less than nothing
Searching for substance – Searching for essence"

And there was another one, apparently called "Who left me here?" (It was hand-written at the top of the page):

"Who left me here?
You left me there
A victim of chance
Destiny and circumstance
Retreat and retrieve
Comply and believe
Fighting for a better place
The volatile that always stays

Break my bones and break my back
Love is the only thing I lack
Watch me leave before I pack
Surrendering slowly before I attack

You left me here
Could have left me anywhere
A victim of your cold
And heartless way of growing old

Reply and relive
All those things you'll never give
Dreaming of a better time
When being in love is not a crime

Break my bones and break my back
Love is the only thing I lack
Watch me return before I go
Going, going, gone so slow"

Mary found them peculiar but interesting. She had never been a fan of poetry as such, but still considered herself an open-minded woman. She realized straight away that she also felt very proud that this had been written by her son. In fact, this was the first, albeit indirect, contact they'd ever had! She re-read them and found new things. Very peculiar. The last one made her a bit sad, as it was so apparently the voice of someone who felt abandoned.

Mary immediately sat down to reply. She felt energized, sad, happy and confused at the same time. She knew that whatever was happening was going to change her life, but it was something she just had to do, no question about it. She had to know more about her son.

"Dear Rama,

I was so happy to hear from you, and happy that I wrote you in the first place. I'm so SORRY for having been silent for such a long time. Life took over. I've led a MISERABLE life after Nepal and from time to time my longing to know things has driven me crazy. At times, I thought everything was a dream, sometimes good, sometimes bad. Please, let's stay in touch from now on. I will do my best, I promise.

You have no idea where he is now?

I hope and pray he is alright, wherever he is.

Write back soon. Very soon. I need to know more.

Love, Mary"

In her mind, Mary already made plans to go back. She had quit working, she had money enough after her parents if she was smart about it. She had been and she still was. Now Mary felt it was time to see the world again, the world she'd left behind such a long time ago without really understanding why.

She started checking out travel routes, costs, all the necessary arrangements, and told no one about it. Not that anyone could stop her, but she just felt it essential to keep this a secret. Her own secret. She tried to remain calm and go through everything in her mind, weighing the pros and cons. As if this could be weighed at all! With every day that passed, she became more and more convinced. There was no way back but to go back. Come what may, she had to act according to her intuition and to the motherhood she had so completely suppressed.

Mary searched the Internet for information on Victor. There was quite a bit, mainly having to do with his music and photography. She found web sites that showed his photos and others where you could hear his music. She was impressed that he had achieved such a lot, but she wasn't really sure that she liked all of it. She liked art, but a lot of Victor's material was hard, almost martial. Mary found interviews from different stages of his development, and printed them out from her computer. The binder acting as a scrapbook grew and she realized she was already a proud mother – again.

The days passed into weeks but Mary was sure that another letter from Nepal would show up. And it did.

"Dear Mary,

Bliss and love and greetings from Nepal to you, Dear One.

You can imagine, I'm sure, how happy we were to hear from you again. We are now in touch and we will remain in touch for as long as you want. No, still no word from Victor. I know where he is though. He's currently in Berlin, Germany, but I think he actually lives in Switzerland or Sweden or some place like that. No address though.

You know, there's one way of getting in touch. We worked very much with him on telepathy. He's very skilled and I remember you had talent too. Try it. Send out some messages. It might work. And if you succeed, please let him know we want him to come back. My dream is to see you both here again, united with us in our daily work and worship. It would be a better place for all of us. And it would mean a great deal to the rest of the world too, believe me.

Write soon, or, even better, come soon. Time is the only nothing that can hold us back. Realize that in yourself and come back soon.

We all love you very much. Rama."

Mary started to cry again. What had she been doing with her life? She was 60, her son was 40, and they had never ever met after her leaving him as a tiny baby. How was this possible? Mary knew she was spaced out when she decided to go back home, but there must have been other things involved too. She found it quite painful to be worshiped as some kind of Hindu goddess but at the same time the people had been so kind to her, the pregnancy, and, later on, to her son Victor – their savior and guru. Remembering it now, it felt like she was phased out by someone else rather than that she had "decided" to go home to the US and lead a miserable life for several decades. At the same time, they had been friendly and had actively tried to persuade her to stay. If Mary was confused in 1971-72, it was nothing compared to what she was right at this moment, holding Rama's letter in her hand.

Added to the letter were some xeroxes of interviews with Victor. There were also some reproduced images of him from these interviews. He was dark blonde, still had blue eyes of course and had apparently developed from a skinny good-looking youth to a quite pouchy middle-aged, bald man. It was weird to see.

Mary looked at the photos she'd kept in her box. Rama was a young man, she herself was young and pretty. And very pregnant. Pictures of people meditating, the mountains and, eventually, of her and her own baby, father unknown.

Crying and going through these old photos and letters, ending in early 1972, just emphasized what Mary already felt. Her entire life was a mystery and a big portion of it a huge illusion. Being in touch with at least a speck of an explanation felt utterly liberating, to say the least.

She lay the photos aside and looked at the xeroxes from Rama.

4

"Interview with Victor Ritterstadt by *The Extreme Underground Gazette*

Q: You are well known in the area of magic. Is this for you more an interest or way of life, which resonates in your various art projects or is traditional ritual magic of concern to you in your daily life?

VR: The most important thing is always to integrate any wisdoms or insights into daily life. Rituals and occultism have no value in themselves to me. I used to be very interested in those topics and have certainly devoted a lot of time to exploring various traditions and schools. But what it all comes down to, at least according to me, is that you have a life and you have a will. If those two aren't united, bad things come. If they are united, on the other hand, miracles will happen. I work hard with trying to stay on the United path.

Q: Aleister Crowley is regarded by most scholars as a "magus", who was basically on a mystic path (in the sense of annihilation of the self). Do you see yourself as a mystic too in that sense, or as a magician?

VR: What can be seen as something of a philosophical conflict between the magical and the mystical, I think can easily be viewed from a kind of Taoist perspective: Why choose between one or the other when you can integrate both? I see no discrepancy or conflict. The concept of "self" is really just a psychological term that's hard to understand. It's all just theories and names anyway.

Q: Satanism is one term that can still really cause much confusion, because it was and still is (besides LeMonde) mostly used in a polemical sense. Do you think "Satanists" use this term just because it fits to the concept or is confusion (frightening people, etc.) part of the "game"?

VR: I have absolutely no interest in confusing or provoking people unless it's necessary – to them. I just do what I feel I have to do. It's strange how certain phenomena and terms are charged with such a potent glamour. I will never deny the inspiration from LeMonde. I'm not on a path where I feel I have to introduce myself with the term or shove it down people's throats. The best thing you can do is, I think, to inspire other people to think and act for themselves.

Q: You seem, like LeMonde, to be fascinated with long forgotten treasures in the area of cinema. What movies have you enjoyed lately? Do you see a certain "power" or indulgence in cherishing alienation and in performing this kind of "occult cultural archaeology"?

VR: I think that one trustworthy navigator in life is resonance. For me, it's OK to feel resonance without having to analyze why I feel the specific resonance. It has to do with aesthetics, childhood memories, significant phases, personal quantum leaps and transformations, etc. Alienation is an interesting thing in this respect. I've found solitude, darkness and silence to be among the most creative states of existence. The feeling of being outside, looking in, has followed me all through my life. Hence, I think, the fascination for voyeurism and weird kinds of anthropology. I'm also a strong believer in the power of talismans. Not necessarily inscribed with demonic or angelic sigils from ancient esoteric lore, but rather just objects, places or whatever that have inspirational power because they've belonged to certain persons or because they've been part of something that means something to you. Art is very potent in this sense – a great non-rational way to leave seeds of change in various places and dimensions. As for movies, it's just obvious: Why waste time on some new computerized epic when you can watch "The Maltese Falcon" or "Sunset Boulevard"? I think the shit around us is becoming so overwhelming, that it's no wonder that watching a movie with real sentiments becomes a sacred act of time travel and reverence.

Q: Magic is of course also often used in a purely aesthetic sense. Why do you think that is and where do you see the relation between Magic and Music, especially as regards your Neuronic Plague-project and your earlier work with Blaxpots?

VR: On an intellectual level, I hope that the material presented will make people go "What do they mean? What's this supposed to be?" or "That's fantastic... I have to check this out!" To be seeds of their own magical development. On an emotional level, I hope the music can conjure atmospheres that are conducive to altered states of mind. Not as escapism, but as interesting and inspiring vibrations to higher explorations within. I think I've looked at things from that perspective all along, in all the music I've been involved in creating, alone or together with other people."

"Interview with Victor Ritterstadt by the *Underneath The Underground Dispatch*

Q: What is that fascinates you with photography?

VR: I really can't explain what's the reason behind my fascination. In essence, I think it's that I belong to the now almost mythical character, "the gatherer". I go on treks, either near or far, and bring back material to my cave. You know, I've been working as a journalist in the same way: traveling, interviewing people and bringing the wisdom or folly home. If you prefer to look at it from a psychological perspective, you could say I'm a voyeur. I like to watch and document at a distance and then draw my own conclusions from my findings. A private kind of anthropology study.

Q: You seem to be very busy man. Writing, making music, photography, etc. Creativity seems to be a very important part of your life.

VR: Yes. Over the years I've certainly had my share of internal struggles about this. Early on, when I was still living in Asia, I decided to follow my own intuition and later on my own will. This could have been fairly easy had my interest or will been limited to one specific thing, like, for instance, writing. But in my case, it's been a mix of writing, taking photos and making music. These parts have been the essence of my life. Now I just live with that, and quite happily so. It's not a bad life after all. One good thing about being diligent and hard working is that as you grow older, there's bound to be, if not fame, then at least infamy. Which means you can attract editors or publishers more easily when it's a matter of the writing. Models, girls, bands, artists, customers, collectors, etc contact you when they've seen your photos, as well as editors and gallery people. And with the music, it's the same there: when people know you exist, they get in touch and want you to come play. That's the main advantage of never giving up and just sticking to your own vision, regardless of whether life is cruel or kind: it's the hard times that give you strength to carry on. And that strength will always lead on to new manifestations.

Q: Is this creative factor connected with any obsessions which drive you in a particular direction? Do they have any common denominator?

VR: Well, I guess you could look at this in many different ways. I don't value psychology highly enough to merely say that "massive manifestation suggests an inferiority complex" or something similar. I believe that psychology is just a very loosely-knit and extremely experimental science, if one dares call it even that. What I do believe though, is that when you have a talent for something, it's your sacred duty to the whole to pursue it and work hard with it. One can refine and develop one's qualities indefinitely, but one can never really become a different person. My need for manifestation I think more has to do with the fact that I like to work a lot and I like to see things manifested, in books, magazines, records, exhibitions etc. It's become a lifestyle. I do hope that whatever it is I do can inspire people too.

If you're smart, do something smart, if you're beautiful, do something that displays the beauty, if you're musically talented, you simply have to make music... It's as simple as that! The only time you can really lose is when you're pretending to be someone else. One should also be careful in constantly evaluating oneself and be honest about the findings and never be concerned about what other people might think. It should be totally irrelevant what other people think or say.

Q: What is the difference between creativity and following schemes and trends in art? Is creativity in a modern, fixed and consolidated cultural pattern possible at all?

VR: Yes, I think so. Basically it has to do with being open to ideas and to the primal energy of creation. I think there are as many, if not more, creative people in other walks of life as in art. The art world is a huge illusion and the idea of an art school is almost preposterous to me. Creative people are those with a passion for a certain thing and who also work very hard with it through an accumulated experience of life. I think that creativity exists all around us and perhaps especially in people you'd never suspect at a first glance. Very few people who've attended art school eventually end up as artists. This has to do with the fact that a direct experience of life is necessary: the fight and struggle of life at its rawest. In a secluded and academic environment this is not possible.

Q: I know you are interested in magic. What is the place of magical arts in a cultural paradigm, in your opinion? Do they create some kind of vital influx in culture? Do they fix a current of cultural development? Or maybe magic is an alternative for all ruling philosophies and cultural trends?

VR: Magic as a phenomenon has undoubtedly been a very marginal thing up until recently. There is definitely an increased interest and a resurgence in real life as well as in its reflection: entertainment. Music, books and movies, to name but a few media, have brought on a huge mass of information and inspiration to look further and deeper. If even only one percent of all the people exposed to this influx are genuinely affected, and actually start treading a path of genuine spiritual development, then that's considerably more than what was the case forty years ago.

What started in the 1960s with the Eastern romance and the drugs have now caught on to something very much more substantial and constructive: young people embrace their own cultural heritage and embrace it in a religious or magical way. For me, this is the only hope for mankind in order not to starve spiritually. I would like to see a greater "heterogenization" of ideas and values. Increased interest in the world is fantastic and home is naturally always where the heart is. But I also think that one always returns home in a physical sense too, meaning not to a specific house, but to a specific culture.

Magic is very hard to define and I don't think that even Aleister Crowley succeeded that well. It's too much of an individual, intuitive thing. But given that if this creative blossom is allowed to grow, whether at night or day, magic is certainly an agent of transformation all through life. Perhaps one definition could be "a directed life force". How people relate to that I can't really say, but I certainly hope that they do.

Q: Is your musical activity connected with any magical experiments?

VR: Certainly. On a philosophical level, we actively work with the union of opposites. We either softly integrate minimal opposites or by force clash two contradicting elements against each other. On a more subdued level, we integrate ideas and concepts we know are seeds, either for personal or for larger flowers that will eventually bloom as a result. Also, in the structures, we like to use things that we know are inspiring or evocative for other people, in their own meditations, listening sessions, trips, etc... Certain sounds, scapes, rhythms, collage effects and so on. That's what really makes the Neuronic Plague a worthwhile experience for me: that it's such a multifaceted tool to work with. We're certainly not a band in the traditional sense.

Q: In this context I'd like to ask you about playing live. What does an ideal relation between musician and audience mean to you?

VR: Here we come to the music technology of today and its inherent advantages as well as drawbacks. There can never be organic interplay between musician and audience if there's no one there to actually physically change the vibrations. I have been hesitant about our live work, as I feel we've been too attached to our computers. That's not a good thing. Things like that affect too, but it can never replace the organic vibrations stemming from one human being to the other. It's almost like a sexual energy that transcends gender concepts. Computers are the condoms of music. You can fuck around as much as you want and you're always safe. But you can never conceive new life. And that's what I think the live shows should be all about: an explosive and vibratory orgy totally fertile and in tune with the harmony of the spheres."

Mary re-read his words many times. Some kind of image gradually grew inside her mind. Her son was an artist, eloquent and apparently very interested in magical things and ideas. She didn't like the slightly arrogant tone that became predominant at times, but couldn't help being intrigued by that she was linked so closely to the mind that had articulated all these words.

Her dreams that night were basically the same one, over and over: she was a bird flying over landscapes, mountains and forests. Was this really her own dream or was it affected by reading her own journal, where such a dream passage had been mentioned?

5

The next day another thick envelope arrived from Rama. It had been sent from Kathmandu on the same day as the letter. Mary opened it eagerly and looked through the contents. Inside was a transcript of some kind of interview between Victor and someone called "Guru". Victor was apparently thirty one years old when this had taken place. It wasn't a copy of something published but seemed to be a private typescript. The heading was written by hand: "Mind Training".

Victor: Pardon me for appearing confused, weak and not so eloquent.

Guru: At times, self-reflection isn't pretty. Begin in the beginning. If there is such a thing.

Victor: My exaggerated adaptability creates problems in the course of life. One day this, one day that. I question facets of the jewel praised only yesterday. The spirits or inspirations may express compensatory needs, but on the whole I see it as quite a hampering phenomenon. I think I need a closer contact with the core identity and its view of the will.

Guru: And here it is. Impressions and inspiration aren't necessarily a problem. It's not necessarily a negative thing or a counter productive phenomenon. However, the main problem seems to be one of constructing, through these forces/agents, methods that are not necessarily the most constructive ones.

Victor: Of this I'm painfully aware.

Guru: A good starting point. The relevant question is the simplest one: What is your will?

Victor: Using my impressions and experiences, filtering them and then expressing stimulating ideas and emotions that may or may not inspire other human beings. As summed up in poetry and art, or vice versa. To be free to devote myself to a constant development of my creativity. The following order has been a predominant one: writing, photography, music.

Guru: All well. And well put. The way I see it, your division between the essence and the attribute is an intelligent one, but perhaps also slightly dualistic – perhaps even unnecessarily so. Don't forget that most achievers have very specific goals in mind, something that could be seen, in the light of your matrix, as belonging in the attribute sphere. A clear cut goal is undoubtedly a focusing agent. You have the energy, the awareness, but do you achieve the results you've set out?

Victor: Not always as I once perceived them. But usually they come, sooner or later.

Guru: Aren't you referring to the manifestations of products along the road?

Victor: Possibly. I see what you're getting at. Scattered manifestations, while in fact I desire a development on a higher and less material level.

Guru: Or perhaps even on a higher material level too? Anyway, you can see it if you look closely. The core identity is linked to a core activity. You call it talismanic writing, meta-programmatic creation, etc. Those terms are in themselves your creations but it's never enough to just concoct. You really should demand more of yourself, given the potential you have.

Victor: Suggesting?

Guru: It's not the well structured agenda that develops your life. It's the conscious choices and work with achieving that which is genuine and closest to a spiritual, intuitive path. Blind work is blind work. Retrospectively, it all adds up – especially if you want it to. Here, your focus on the essential becomes a key. Why do you express? Because you know you need to. What do you express? Filtered impressions. But how do you express these? I don't mean that in terms of terms or words, formulations, etc. I mean: How do you express yourself?

Victor: I usually see what's available and use that to my advantage.

Guru: That's an astute observation. But are you certain that's the best method for you?

Victor: Not at all. It's one that I'm accustomed to and one that apparently has resonated well with my neurotic imprints.

Guru: Alright then. One could say that you take what is given to you, that you are content with what's readily available, that you "make do" with fairly easy solutions. I wonder if it wouldn't be better on all levels if you looked at everything from a different angle. An angle where you are the great arbiter and the analyst and you are the decision-maker and the holder of the great scales. Where your will, intelligence, emotional needs and creativity all work together to achieve a desired result. You know you can handle the path on your own. Your quota of impressions is filled for the time being. You have more than enough inside to open up and hand out well-formulated portions in various ways.

Victor: I question the link to the Order, to the Neuronic Plague and similar structures. They are, according to your suggestion, constructs that in many ways create easy solutions but perhaps not the completely desired ones.

Guru: Correct. What you feel an emotional need of having projected at or on you is not necessarily what is closest to your genuine will. Why desire to be looked upon as an interesting and experimental musician or artist (in the Neuronic Plague context) when you don't feel a need to create experimental music as soon as you wake up? Somehow, I sense a discrepancy here. And the Order? Isn't that merely a pretext for being able to sleep at people's places when traveling? Relationships which construct even more invisible links and demands? Sometimes the hospitality is greater and more genuine in a hotel, where you're really free to do what you like.

Victor: I'm painfully aware of all these interpretations. I have created many imaginary castles made up of solutions that have perhaps not been entirely thought through. The aspect of freedom becomes evident. What appears to be freedom in actual fact becomes traps and chains, but on another level.

Guru: Absolutely correct. Freedom and will are, as you so well know, ultimate arbiters in your life. Freedom is having choices, but that doesn't imply that those choices have to be made, in the sense that they all must be tasted whimsically. To put it more concretely: you can essentially never be more free than when you're writing. It's a freedom to create – and thereby, by proxy, manifest – that doesn't really demand more than focus and something to write with. To arrange for an environment in space and time in which to write is the ultimate challenge of freedom for you. Thereby, the construct of "needing money" or this or that is in many ways just a vague desire. Formulation is quintessential. Freedom, creation, freedom to create freedom to create, etc, is really what it's all about. So that's where you need to be. Daily anxieties of practical or other natures have a tendency to become diversions through their daydreaming potential.

Victor: And here we return to the spirits or inspirations that seem to fill me with constructive energy but perhaps actually counteract an optimal development.

Guru: Again, what you need to do is formulate well. On project levels, on personal levels, on emotional levels. It's the core identity that expresses and it needs to be done in your voice and through your spirit. When you sit down to write, it needs to be in your words. You have enough inspiration, and you can tap that by just focusing on the writing in itself.

Victor: I have a tendency to let life as such take over and create emotional diversions. This in turn creates muddled desires based on reactive patterns.

Guru: Correct. Say “No” or “I'd rather” rather than “Yes, of course” or “Yes, why not?” Now that you have tasted temporal freedom and have experimented with it, you can take that much further. The creativity shouldn't be part of your structure but rather vice versa. Things can wait, people can wait, secondary phenomena can wait. If you really value your creativity as you should, then that means putting it first in your priorities. Small scale strategies take large scale time and effort. Evaluate and decide and just be very frank about it. I think you have wasted enough time. This has only been based on your indecisions or the fact that you have a hard time possibly or actually being disliked. But everyone likes a winner. And a winner is someone who gets to the goal, who manifests what he has set out to manifest.

Victor: One source of constant frustration is of course my own knowledge of all these things.

Guru: Knowledge is never, properly speaking, a source of frustration. It's that you don't act upon that knowledge that's frustrating. It's an entirely different matter. You are aware of who you are and what you can do. Yet you doubt! That's something you should be ashamed of. You have to be much more consequent in your decision-making and your actions henceforth. Be what you are. Be who you are. To settle for less is to create an unworthy situation.

Victor: Other people's opinions or, worse still, presumed opinions, have played their part in this. That's something I'm ashamed of.

Guru: Understandable. To be very concrete again... As for the writing, focus on one project at a time, according to your wit.

Disregard attribute-based fantasies about results and results of the results. Write, produce and immerse yourself in intuitive and intelligent creation in an eloquent way. The process. By all means, photograph, paint, make music, but don't do it based on attribute-based fantasies. The actual results will speak their own language and will attract the relevant attention needed for prosperity and advancement. Results not stemming from an essential force are unable to attract a proper attention. You are the one who wants to advance and make progress, but that's not possible if the work is not communicated in your own language. The water always finds its own level.

Victor: I'm concerned about my livelihood and the finances needed. I feel that I position myself in the worst possible way when it comes to money and that it relates to psychic and emotional ties and patterns that are beyond my control – or so it seems. It is an area of great concern.

Guru: You absolutely need to use your creativity in more ways than mere artistic production. I agree, this is a dilemma for you mainly because it's a habit, a pattern. See yourself from the outside: 31 years old, intelligent, creative. Why is it that you can't support yourself? Why is it that you can't manifest your own freedom?

Victor: A negative symbiosis with my non-existing mother, I'd say. You know that. As for my father, who knows? You yourself said that God is my father.

Guru: That's one explanation that you've been quick to use in your own psycho-analytical work. But a good explanation can also, especially in your case, contain devious diversions. I'm not saying the explanation is altogether untrue. But there is more to this than meets the eye. Remember freedom? Freedom is having choices. What choices do you have in terms of supporting yourself? Actually, quite many. Like getting a job for instance.

Victor: This would interfere with my creative freedom when this is applied to, for instance, actual writing and reading. It takes time. I fear it would drain me.

Guru: Listen well: The fear is based in an unwillingness to be in charge of your own selections. A job isn't necessarily something that is imposed upon you and something that is all draining and negative. Why settle for that? The energy you spend on worrying about these things could be spent on something profitable instead. You are very quick to assume the worst. No doubt an inheritance from your relationship to your mother. What about that umbilical cord? It needs to be cut and I advise you not to wait. You need to break free as of this moment. You break free not by dramatic measures and emotional reactivity, but simply by making your own money. Now, here's the challenge... How can you turn your creativity into profitability? Listen carefully: It will not debase your creativity. It will not destroy any concepts of "purity" that you may have. The concepts don't exist other than as mere concepts. You need to address life in work and action. A piece of advice: synchronicities and synergies appear when you've earned them."

6

Mary inserted these papers into her binder. There was a lot to digest in what Victor said in these papers. Although slightly pompous at times, he said things that were relevant. It was rich material. She flipped through the pages again. It struck her as strange that she had never researched him on the Internet during all these years. It was as if there had been a heavy veil on top of her and on top of everything that had anything to do with those Nepalese days.

She realized that there was really no turning back now. She needed to get back to Nepal. She needed to be in contact with this strange man that was her son. If he felt the same way was hard to tell, but it didn't really matter to Mary. If she didn't act now, she would never know. Know what?, she asked herself. Even that, an exact answer, seemed superficial and irrelevant to her. The main thing to do now was to act.

In the quiet of that afternoon, Mary lit some candles and some incense she had bought at a new age bookstore. She looked around the room. It was nice. The room was clean, there was something serene about the atmosphere. She sat down on the floor and started getting into her own meditation routines: breathing and movements that hadn't been part of her since Nepal. But now they were back, just like that, and it felt overwhelmingly good. Mary smiled for the first time in a long while.

She sat cross-legged in silence and gazed at the room. The subdued light from the candles and the sweet aroma of the incense made her perceptions less sharp-edged, yet more alert.

"Dearest Victor...", she whispered. "If you're there... If you're there, somewhere, please let me know... This is your mother trying to get in contact with you..."

Mary realized that this was probably pretty insane, bur decided to spend at least half an hour doing it. And she did.

Victor Ritterstadt lay in his bedroom in Berlin. He slept heavily and dreamt vividly of desert vistas and heat. He felt alone but the sense of adventure compensated for the loneliness. While wandering barefoot over the dunes, he could suddenly hear a voice.

"If you're there please let me know...", a woman's voice said.

Victor didn't know what to make of it. The voice interfered with his dream. The desert suddenly seemed like a mirage, fading out.

"Sure, I'm here. Who wants to know?", Victor replied and sat down on the scorching desert sand.

"It's me, your mother... Is that really you?"

Victor was startled by the announcement and felt he wanted to wake up properly. Before he did so, he told her to come back in twenty-four hours. Then he woke up in a cold sweat, a far cry from the hot desert he'd been exploring just a minute ago. As he woke up, he remembered the very last bits. He took notice of the time and decided that he must be better prepared the next time.

Mary got up from the floor of her living room. She might have been mistaken, but she had felt that there was indeed someone there on the other side. She didn't know what to make of it but decided to try again in twenty-four hours. She didn't know why, but it somehow felt appropriate to trust her gut feeling. From now on, she was going to trust all those hunches.

7

Twenty-four hours later, Mary was back in her cross-legged position on the floor. Victor was back asleep. He'd made sure that he'd be extra tired that night too, by reading a lot and taking a long walk through the Berlin Zoo.

Mary began in the same way, by calling for him. It did take some time, perhaps ten minutes, before she felt that exhilarating tingle again. There was indeed someone there on the other side, wherever that was.

"Is that you, Victor? This is your mother..."

"I'm here. I'm not awake, not asleep, but I'm here... Where are you? I'm in Berlin."

"I'm just outside New York, in America."

Mary had no trouble whatsoever to send and receive formulated sentences. It was as if she were speaking and listening as usual, although in complete silence.

"It's strange to hear from you. Have you been in touch with Rama?", Victor asked.

"Yes. I have been very sad. Very tired. Going crazy. I need to go back. I need to be in contact with you", she said.

"It's OK", Victor replied. "I don't mind at all. I have been angry at times, but I'm not anymore. Life is what it is. It also is what we make of it. I don't mind you being there at all."

"I'm very happy to hear that...", Mary said and felt her tears coming. "Very happy. I don't know where to begin. I am so sorry."

"Don't be unless you want to", Victor said. "I bear no ill will. I used to think it was your fault but it's impossible to say that. Perhaps all the good things I've experienced have been thanks to your not being there and not because of it, in a negative way? Do you follow? I guess it's a matter of perspective most of all... I'm sorry, I'm about to wake up... Twenty-four hours again... Twenty-four hours..."

Mary opened her eyes. She had a hard time believing that she had just been in telepathic contact again with her son. But she accepted it as fact rather than fantasy. This filled her with strength to start planning for her Asian trip before she finally went to bed early that night, exhausted but overjoyed.

When she woke up the next morning she spent about an hour trying to locate a telephone number for Rama. This was hard work, as she didn't know his real or last name, and "Rama" was probably around in the millions. Eventually, she did track down a number for the Patanjali Yoga Retreat Center, just north of Kathmandu.

She dialed the number to Nepal. After a couple of signals, a woman's voice could be heard, slightly disturbed by static.

"Hello? My name is Mary Ritterstadt and I wonder if Rama is there, please?"

"Hold on... Do you wish to book a retreat? Have you been here before?", the woman inquired.

"Actually, yes, but this is more of a personal nature", Mary continued.

"I see. Rama won't be back until tomorrow morning. Can I take a message?"

"Yes, tell him Mary called from America. He knows me. I hope so. I think I've found a person we're both looking for... I'll call back."

"OK, thanks... I'm just curious... Is this person your son? Your name is Mary?"

"Yes, that's me. I'll call back later then, OK?"

"No", the woman said. "Please hang on. Don't hang up. Hang on."

A short time passed and Mary could hear human voices filtered through the phone line static.

"Mary?", a man's voice asked, with a distinct Nepalese accent.

"Yes", Mary answered. "This is she. Is that Rama?"

"Mary! Mary! How wonderful! Yes, Rama is here! How wonderful. Please say something..."

"Hello..."

"Yes, Hello! Hello, yes! Oh Mary, Mary... Are you coming here now?"

"I think so. I want to. But wait, Rama, listen... I have been in touch with Victor."

"Ah, even better! Have his number? You call him?"

"No, telepathy... At least I think so."

"Wonderful! Mary, I'm so happy. You come now and you tell him he must come too. We have waited so long. Too long now.

You will be happy here. Please, please come, Mary, and take him with you."

"Well, it's not like he's a little boy anymore, Rama. Also, I'm in America and he's in Europe."

"No matter, no matter. Come here and come here soon. Please give me your telephone number, Mary. And please give Victor our number too."

Mary's state of excitement grew more and more elevated. From having been depressed and morose, she was now in flux and joy. She was going, no doubt about it, and she wanted to meet Victor and see if all of this was reality or just a pleasant dream. She needed to establish a better contact with him first though and perhaps get the phone number for him too.

8

The same routine followed later on. They were in contact more or less immediately. Victor preferred to do telepathy while slightly hypnagogue, so the time frame was perfect for this. Not dreaming and not having to dose off while being fully awake, he was now, in the small hours of the Berlin morning, totally receptive to telepathic transmissions.

"So here we are...", Mary said.

"Yes. Have you been in touch with Rama?"

"Yes. He wants me to come back. He wants you to come back."

"OK. I'm not opposed to it. I need some change."

"What are you working on?", Mary wondered.

"Writing, photos, some music... Sometimes one by one, sometimes together... I don't know. It's just what I do..."

"What do you take pictures of, Victor?"

"I guess... Life, today... Nothing special... Just scenes and atmospheres... They turn into writing later on. The camera is a sketchbook, you know. Well, for me at least."

"It sounds interesting. I have seen some of your stuff on the Internet. It looks so good. I would sure like to see the photos for real some day."

"Maybe. Maybe I've burnt all the negatives? In many ways

I have. But I have to admit I'm too attached to all those images. But they're still just fragments. Like 'life-today-thickeners'. Know what I mean?"

"Sure, but they're fragments of your life, Victor. They're valuable. Let's not talk any more about this now. Are you going to come to Nepal or not?"

"I'm thinking about it, as we communicate. I just fear that it'll be a big hoopla when I get there. And if you come too. You know, first having to face you, and..."

"Thanks, that wasn't very nice."

"Sorry, I didn't mean it just like that. But try to see it from my point of view. We haven't really met, ever. Yet you are my mother. As far as I understand, we're both either victims of an American psychedelic rock group, America's then – in many ways – most wanted renegade chemist, a brainwashing Hindu love cult or, who knows, maybe we are living gods. Can you understand why I'm slightly hesitant about going back to Nepal?"

9

Inside an anonymous-looking building on the outskirts of Berlin, a woman of some thirty years, Ilse Grokmann, began her night shift. She sat down by her desk, mainly filled with computer equipment. She looked through the notes of her colleague, who she'd caught sleeping at work, again. It happened to her too at times. The job was quite slow and only very rarely did something happen. She looked forward to another calm night and had, disobeying the rules herself, again, brought a copy of Tolstoy's Anna Karenina.

After just fifteen minutes of illicit Tolstoyean pleasures Grokmann's escapism was disturbed. She noticed discrepancies on one of her computer screens. There was something going on there. She put on headphones. Yes, there was a signal there, unmistakably. She looked at the screen and followed a live feed of a little red symbol that jumped up and down.

"Götterdämmerung", she said to herself. "This is strong stuff."

After making sure that the capture of all this activity was working, she reached for a telephone.

"Hello? This is Ilse Grokmann at Telelabs. Yes, fine thank you. Yes, no... Something is going on here and it's strong. I think you'd better come on over."

Half an hour later Professor Friedrich Schopenbaur showed up, tired but curious. He was head engineer at Telelabs and, like the younger Grokmann, used to a slow, comfortable and government-funded pace.

"What's going on?", he asked her.

"I had a clear transmission for fifteen minutes. Between humans. A communication, that is. Two people sending and receiving."

"You're absolutely certain?", Schopenbaur asked her.

"Absolutely. Have a seat and I'll play it back."

He sat down, looked and listened. Then he looked up at his assistant.

"Götterdämmerung, this is strong stuff."

"I know", Grokmann said. "Strongest I've seen."

"Give me a print-out please. I have some people to call."

Schopenbaur's call caused quite a stir. At similar offices around the world, there was either the direct report from Schopenbaur or tapped and slightly distorted versions of it. Small groups in Washington, DC, London, England, Brussels, Belgium, Moscow, Russia and just outside Beijing in China gathered to look at the data. The assessment was about the same in each place, but best summed up by NATO General Unter-Oberst in Brussels:

"This is something out of the ordinary. I want a field agent on this right away. The main sender is in Germany, so get someone over there right away. Track everything, break into Telelabs, whatever... We need to know who's doing this. And why. And, yes, how!"

Schopenbaur knew what was coming and activated his advanced scrambling devices in the walls of Telelabs. They also declined sudden visits by salesmen, consultants and bug exterminators. Instead, his entire team was called in, plus some intelligence officers from a German organization which didn't really exist (and still doesn't). Together they looked at the material back and forth and back again. It was beyond doubt: they were witnessing a record of possibly the clearest telepathic communication they'd ever seen. It even seemed that it was intercontinental. The implications of this were, as they used to say jokingly at Telelabs, beyond words.

"I've tuned everything to the same frequency", Grokmann began. "If it happens again and if it's in the same range, we'll be able to find the one that's here. More or less. I hope so, anyway. Maybe."

"That's excellent", Schopenbaur said. "Certainty is the foundation of our science. I just hope it happens again."

"Could it be terrorists?", one of the intelligence officers, Schwarzenberg, asked him.

"Possibly. Usually, we only have freak occurrences, like strong dreams that are received by another person, but usually very close by. We have caught some of that. But it's always a jumble, like dreams often are. We have been able to fine-tune our scanning equipment using those freak transmissions. It's gotten us quite far. But this is the stuff we've been waiting for. So, yes, it could very well be terrorists. If we only had more funding, we could..."

"Alright, we'll talk about that later", the agent interrupted. "But what you're saying is that you've never really experienced this?"

"Not like this, no. In our lab downstairs, we've experimented with silent communication and it's been very successful so far. Right, Ilse?"

Ilse Grokmann nodded. She remembered the experience between Schopenbaur and herself, in which she was to receive his silent transmission. They were staring at each other a long time at first, then with closed eyes. Her mind became full of images and scenes, in which she was slowly sodomized by Schopenbaur. When the experiment was over, he asked her to be totally honest in her recounting of what had happened. She told him shyly exactly what she had "received". And Schopenbaur, happy as a child, jumped with joy and conveyed to her that it had indeed been an altogether accurate transmission.

"How does it work?", the agent asked. "You're tapping into the mobile phone networks?"

"All the networks", Schopenbaur said proudly. "Mobile phones, satellites, radio, Ethernet, wireless internet, any net, all the frequencies. We can monitor and measure everything now.

Telepathy has a very distinct frequency, you see. It has to do with brainwaves. Brainwaves directed by will. The brain as will and representation of a human being's desire to communicate without words."

"I'm just curious", the agent continued. "How much has this cost?"

"Approximately 60 million Euro is what I've received for my research", Schopenbaur sighed. "But it's not enough. Far from it."

"I'll tell you something. If we get hold of this fucking terrorist, you can be sure to get some more funding for your project. If he or they can transmit thoughts, images and sentences into people's minds, who knows what's next?"

Ilse Grokmann dreaded the thought, taking into account that Schopenbaur transmitted "thoughts" to her quite often. She silently wondered what was going to happen next in Anna Karenina.

10

Mary waited and waited for something to show up the next afternoon. Victor had been there as usual, at the same time, but perhaps he was becoming arrogant, promising things he couldn't or simply wouldn't honor. She let an hour pass by, just thinking about him. She started feeling the buzz in her mind and breathed deeply.

"Is that you, Victor?"

"Yes. Sorry, but I had to do some other stuff. I'm actually wide awake now, and not hypnagogue at all. I hope you can receive this clearly. Here's a little thing I wrote for you last night. If you want a key to why I do what I do, then this is it. Here goes...

If I could travel anywhere
I would travel everywhere
One endless trip
With occasional stops
To assemble the documentation
Escapism is just another word

For the Eternal Return
The Eternal Return
To my own Locus Solus
My mind's settling down
To its own given balance
There is also destiny
A given point and given time
Masters, gods and puppeteers
Invisible timelords
I am a mere chroniclerk
But, as such, a free man
Free to return once more
To wherever I choose
Leaving spiritual footprints
Behind and in front
Of the time I'm in
And will be once again
There is also destiny
A frame of reference
A frame of an image
That has yet to be created
Yet to be interpreted
Yet to be torn apart
To be fully integrated
Art and spirit
Fodder for the soul's revelation
Revealing one's own strengths
And others' weaknesses
Stand fast in the Quagmire of opinions
A branch to grasp for
Only grows from the hearts
Of the very real imaginists
Those with integrated
Psycho-geometrical designs
That are theirs and theirs alone
Alone
Only time will tell
Only history will judge
All footprints are eventually erased

From babies' minds
All one has to do
And actually can do
Is start over
Solvitur Ambulando
Make me see what you do
Make me do what you see
A particular vision
Containing no regrets
Ultimatums, promises or fulfillments
It really is playback time
And we all share the same
Cerebral membrane
Sensitive to influence
If I could travel anywhere
I would travel everywhere
Assume power focus
Fade to indifference
Let go
Walk
Think
Fast
Wait
Think
Fast
Wait
Walk
Let go"

Mary opened her eyes slowly, just a little. The transmission seemed to be over. She still wanted more though. This poem or whatever it was meant to be was really good, she thought and closed her eyes again.

"Baby? Are you there?", she whispered.

"Don't call me baby. Did you listen?"

"Yes, it was great."

"I know it's great. But did you listen?"

"Of course…"

"I think that the more primordial and raw the expression is, the more refined and adept the artist in question is. We're living in an era of narcissistic ironic mirror-art, mere self reflections with a certain sense of wit. Art should rather be subtle or brutal explosions of will, intent and life force, if you ask me!"

"I don't know what to say."

"That's your problem. It really is. As for me, I can write myself out of or into anything. By the way, I wrote something else just for you too last night."

"Oh?"

"Yeah. I was thinking about you and it wasn't all bad actually. Do you want to hear it?"

"Of course… Wait…", Mary said and lay down comfortably and relaxed. This was going to be good.

"OK, here goes…", Victor began. "How does one carry on in the spirit of psychedelic illumination without being called an old hippie? I have no idea. How does one bring about radical, personal change for others to take further? I haven't got a clue. How does one come to terms with the fact that the most grand and overwhelming changes all stem from subtle and quite often invisible sources and forces? I have no say in the matter.

When you try to describe the essentially indescribable, there's always the looming danger of becoming a missionary. And the missionary position is not necessarily the best one.

It's never a question of specific vested interests or even of control of the masses. Let's not get paranoid. Let's not get frightened. Let's not get lost. It is however a question of a more profound quality. The one that constitutes the essence of what most people call their bad conscience. That quality is called honesty. You know what it means: Your own relationship to truth. If everyone were honest, the world would be a very different place, wouldn't you agree?

If we go beyond the enjoyable trip trappings, the sensuous neon lights of the soul, the creation of eternities in fragments of seconds, the upheaval of space dissolved in one human sublingual metabolism, one thing remains. It always remains: The challenge to embrace honesty."

"Wow, that's so great. Wow! Thanks. I really liked it.", Mary said.

There was silence. He was gone again.

"Hello?"

Silence. Mary wondered if this was an intentional silence from his side or just a glitch in their telepathy? Next time, there would have to be some kind of telephone number. Just to see if this was at all real or not.

11

Grokmann and Schopenbaur stuck to themselves at the office that night. They monitored, recorded and had the telepathic conversation printed out. They understood that this was no longer a possible benevolent random mishap in experimental science, but a severe breakthrough in advanced mind research. Grokmann was by now truly impressed by Schopenbaur and his vision, as was Schopenbaur himself.

Their ecstatic isolation was an illusion though. While they had been out to lunch in the daytime, a team of (non-existing) agents had inserted relay-modems in all the computers, so that everything that went on, also went on in similar computers in a nearby monitoring van.

On a higher level, people in charge had been in agreement to share this revolutionary intelligence with like minds in other friendly governments. Along the way, all of it leaked too, so like minds of not so friendly governments could also take part of Victor's psychedelic poetry. The consensus was that this was very dangerous material indeed. Dangerous to whom or to what just hadn't been decided yet.

12

Mary wrote to Rama about her plans, and also thanked him for suggesting the telepathy experiment with Victor. She stressed that she wasn't really sure yet when she'd come but would write back as soon as she knew. She knew she would probably call him again before the letter had reached him anyway, but it didn't matter to her. She just wanted to be in touch again, in as many ways as possible

That very same afternoon, Victor and Mary exchanged phone

numbers via telepathy. They agreed that she should call the number in Berlin right away. After having written it down, she gradually left her mild trance state and dialed a number for Berlin, Germany.

"Yes, hello?"

"It's me. Is that you?", Mary asked.

"Indeed it is...", Victor replied. "This is pretty magnificent, right? It was all for real... You had some doubts, right?"

Mary started crying. It was overwhelming. Not only the telepathy business, that it had actually worked, but that she was speaking to her own son for the first time.

"Do you want to talk or cry?", Victor asked.

"A little bit of both...", Mary sobbed.

"OK. Fair enough. Where should we begin? Let's get some steam out of the system first. I want to say that I don't really hate you."

Mary could express nothing but muted sobs.

"I take that as an affirmation that you heard what I said. Mind you, I have hated you. A lot. But that's over now. I can't really blame you for everything that's been going on. We're all responsible for ourselves in the end."

"Victor... This is so fantastic... First Rama and now you... I can hardly believe it...", Mary said and tried to wipe her face and blow her nose at the same time.

"Sure. I understand. I've put those Nepalese weirdos aside for a long time now. They want me back."

"I know", Mary said. "They want me to come on over too. Would you mind? I would so much like to meet you."

"OK. Yes, maybe. I've been doing OK without them and I have certainly done OK without you. But I agree it could be interesting to see what happens."

"Interesting? Is that all?"

"That's quite enough. Please don't expect me to become all sappy and all-embracing just because you're my mother. So what? You're a complete stranger, and always have been."

Mary started sobbing again. Although she enjoyed talking to Victor, it was at the same time immensely painful.

"That said, I'm not entirely opposed to us meeting. Where are you at now? New York?"

"I'm just outside New York. And you're in Berlin?"

"Yes. Well, temporarily at least. Are you actually free to go to Nepal?", Victor asked.

"Yes. I'm retired. I can go there basically anytime. How about you?"

"Free as the wind, more or less."

When the call was over, Mary was exhausted. She kept crying. She sat down on a chair with her hands covering her face and just let the tears fall. She was happy that all of this was happening but couldn't figure out just why it was happening right now. Very soon she realized why though. It was quite simply because she had wanted it to happen.

13

Victor had recently finished some business in Berlin, which meant he was free to move about again. He often went on small trips, to celebrate his freedom and to take photos and write while on the road. At the moment there was absolutely nothing that tied him up in Berlin, so he decided to travel down to Croatia. He'd been there before and liked it a lot. It was close enough, inexpensive and, most important of all, very different.

As he packed his camera gear, some books and some clothes, he thought that perhaps he should let his mother know about his plans, now that they were in more or less regular touch. But he shrugged it off as absurd. It hadn't been any of her business before, and that's how it was going to remain. And, anyway, now that their emotional telepathy worked and seemed to get stronger, that would surely work in Croatia too.

14

Victor drifted through Zagreb's old town with a camera in his hand. As soon as he found something of interest or attraction, he snapped away. The more intuitive, the better, he thought. He drifted on, aimlessly, kept looking around, approached the main square and wound up down by the central station.

He knew from experience that areas of suspense, with people in states of emotional anticipation, were always rich and varied. People waiting, coming, going backwards or forwards in uncertain limbo. Victor had hundreds, if not thousands, of photographs of people in this kind of in betweenness. Definitely a magical state of mind to be in, he thought.

He moved slowly through crowds, taking pictures very discretely. Everybody was busy with something else or nothing else, their eyes scanning crowds, faces, spaces and human patterns. Victor loved to capture these fleeting moments without really knowing why. But, then again, that was the whole point: to not know why and to immerse himself in chance to the greatest extent possible. In his mind, trying to find out why he worked as he worked would equal a form of sacrilege. All these faces, all these situations, all these moments are small pieces of a mosaic of an understanding that is neither retinal, rational nor intellectual, he thought. If he would deny himself even one moment of this creative compulsion, he would be denying himself the ability to get closer to a state of pure chance.

Just as Victor was about to enter the café at the station, he caught a glimpse of something that made him stop. Or, rather, someone. Slightly backlit, he could see a young woman, probably just over twenty, holding a rose and quite obviously waiting for someone. To Victor, it almost looked like a religious image. The sun was bathing the young woman in a warm light and he could even see the dirt and dust floating in the air around her. It was a sad image, because she was still waiting, still looking. Victor took a quick picture of her as she scanned the platform for a familiar face.

She was pretty, Victor thought. Brown hair, dark eyes, slightly big but beautifully proportioned. Without hesitating, Victor went over to her.

"Excuse me, do you speak English?", Victor asked her.

"Sure", she answered, still looking out over the platform. "Why?"

"Isn't he coming?", Victor continued.

"Who?"

"The guy you're waiting for..."

Victor realized it must have sounded totally corny, like some kind of second-rate pick-up line, which is essentially what it was.

"I'm waiting for my aunt, actually", the woman said. "But something's not right. The train came and left. No sign of her."

"Let's have a coffee and wait then", Victor suggested. "There's a café right there."

"Go ahead", she said. "I'm going to make some calls first. I'll join you in a little while. And if you're not there then, don't worry."

"Oh no, I'll be there. See you soon."

Victor got a table by the window, overlooking the platforms. He looked at her, still backlit and almost moving in slow motion. She was talking into a mobile phone and making small gestures.

Why had he approached her? He had no idea, at least not on any rational level. Attraction? Sure, she was pretty to him, but there was more to this too. He knew it. He had never been an impulsive Casanova-type and this moment wouldn't change that. Or would it?

"Thanks for waiting", she said as she joined him. "She'll be on the next train. I have to wait. I'm Veronica, by the way."

"Victor."

They shook hands and started smiling like shy teenagers. A waiter came by. They ordered double espressos.

"Nice to meet you", Victor said.

"Nice to meet you too."

"Are you from Zagreb?"

"Not at all. I'm from Macedonia. I'm going back with my aunt. She's been here on business. I just joined her."

"So you're going back soon?", Victor asked and Veronica nodded slowly.

"How about you? Where are you from?"

"Well, to make a long story short, I'm from Nepal and Germany", Victor replied.

"Oh really? I love Germany. Where exactly?"

"Berlin."

"So you're going back to Berlin?"

"At some point yes, but not now. I'm here to... Just be here. Take some pictures, do a bit of writing."

"That sounds great", Veronica said. "Nice camera. You take a lot of pictures?"

"At times. I write mainly though, but the photos help me remember things, details, faces... It's like a notebook for pictures. What about you?"

The waiter brought the coffees and Veronica moved the camera to another chair.

"I teach French to kids", she continued. "It's OK but usually some kids do everything to disturb the ones who really want to learn."

"It's always like that, isn't it?", Victor continued. "There's always that element of assholeism wherever you go."

"Assholeism? That's a good word", Veronica said, smiling.

"By all means, keep it. Listen, when do you think you'll be leaving?"

"If my aunt is on the next train, and I hope she is, we'll be able to catch the afternoon train to Belgrade and then the night train from there to Skopje. I think the train leaves here at 4.30. Why?"

"This might sound a bit crazy, but..."

"Try me", she said.

"I'd like very much if I could... If I could..."

"Have sex with me?", Veronica laughed.

"Yes, that too. But first, actually, if I could join you? I mean, to go with you to Macedonia?

"Are you some kind of madman?", Veronica asked.

"Absolutely."

"Then yes, you're more than welcome to join me and auntie. She'll be confused of course but that is just normal. It doesn't matter."

"Great. I'll go to my hotel now and check out. And get the ticket. So it's 4.30 this afternoon? Skopje via Belgrade?"

Veronica nodded.

15

Victor took a taxi to the hotel and packed his clothes and books in a rush. In the midst of it all, he realized that he'd forgotten his camera at the café. It made him angry at first, as it was one of his favorite cameras, a Leica from the 1970s. Not the most expensive camera he had, but an important one – it had been a gift from someone special in Nepal who had more or less entrusted it to him.

He knew it would be irrational to just rush back immediately. Better to finish everything properly. After packing, he checked out and took a taxi back to the station. The waiter at the café showed no sign of recognition, either of him, Veronica or a lost camera. Victor went over to the ticket offices instead, disgruntled but determined to continue in his adventure anyway.

"One ticket for Skopje via Belgrade on the 4.30, please."

"You mean 3.30?", the woman behind the counter replied.

"Eh, no, the one 4.30."

"The train for Macedonia leaves at 3.30. You change in Belgrade to the night train. Do you want a ticket or not?"

Victor got his ticket and looked around him. What was going on? Had his young beauty set him up in order to steal his beloved Leica camera? It didn't make sense.

Victor looked at his watch. Just after 3. He walked towards the platform. No sign of Veronica. Oh well, I've never been to Macedonia, so what the hell, he thought. And he did have an extra camera in his well-worn leather backpack.

The train rolled in and he found his compartment. He looked out his window. No Veronica. In a way, he admired her audacity. What a sly little thief! As the train started to move, he even laughed at his own gullibility. He shut the window. As he turned around, suddenly there she was, standing in the compartment doorway.

"Ta-da! Special camera delivery!", she laughed and handed him the Leica.

They hugged for a long time.

"I thought you'd tricked me...", Victor began.

"Why on earth would I trick you? I know I said the wrong time. I'm sorry about that. I didn't have your number. But if I hadn't seen you board this train, I would have stayed until you would have come at 4.30."

"But there is no train at 4.30."

"I know that", Veronica continued. "I was lucky that I stayed at the station. Again, I'm very sorry for the confusion. You said we should meet and now we meet."

"Do you have any idea why we're doing this?", Victor asked.

"No, but I look forward very much to finding out", she answered. "But now I really have to get back to auntie. Why don't we meet later on? By the way, very nice camera. I took some pictures. I hope you don't mind."

They kissed briefly and she left. Victor sat down on his couch. He was happy. Very happy. She really was a sweet girl. His intuition had been right all along. He even had his camera back.

16

Victor was soon joined in the compartment by an old Serbian man who introduced himself as a retired businessman. They each had three seats and hoped it would stay that way, they agreed. The man seemed civilized. He was slim and sinewy, with piercing light-blue eyes and silver-colored hair. He took off his khaki safari jacket and brought out a book.

"History", he told Victor, "very important to know history."

Victor found the man calm and likeable. They both read their books, occasionally looked out the window and at each other, but soon fell asleep.

After six slow-winding hours later, it was time to change trains in Belgrade. They joined forces, as the man was apparently traveling to Macedonia too. They even had the same compartment on the night-train. The man said he'd probably bought his tickets right after Victor, or vice versa. At a distance, he saw Veronica and an older lady. They waved to each other as they boarded the new train.

About an hour after Belgrade, Veronica knocked on the door. Her aunt had finally gone to sleep. The Serbian man looked at them and smiled.

"I go to bistro for thirty minutes. Thirty minutes", he said and left.

Victor and Veronica quickly turned the seats into beds and then embraced, kissed and caressed, disrobing at the same time. A violent charge and arousal followed, of the kind Victor could really only remember from his own prurient teenage fantasies. Veronica was attentive, compliant, devoted. Their swift and sweaty union culminated in a throbbing orgasm and muted screams and sighs from them both.

"I'm so happy I trusted my gut feeling about you", Victor said as they lay on the bed, catching their breaths.

"I'm so happy I trusted my gut feeling about you", Veronica replied. "This was very, very, very nice."

"Very nice indeed. Come on, let's get dressed before the old guy comes back."

"Strange", Veronica said. "He seemed familiar. Ordinary, I know, but there was something about him..."

"You know what?", Victor said. "I wouldn't mind going to the bistro myself. I'm hungry."

"Me too. It sounds like a really good idea."

They kissed, dressed and left the compartment. The old man was nowhere to be seen. Maybe he was in a rest room, Victor thought.

They sat down, tired, hungry, highly in love without knowing why or how. They ordered food, wine and enjoyed each other's company. She had charm, she had wit and was just a pleasure to be with. It turned out that she, too, was interested in cosmic and spiritual things. Victor wasn't surprised at all. They resonated and got a thrill out of being each other's center of attention.

At one a.m. the bistro closed and they walked hand in hand towards his compartment.

"It'd be nice to have you sleep over", Victor said.

"That man was nice but I don't think he'll be that nice", Veronica said and laughed, more than a little tipsy from the wine.

When they entered Victor's car, they immediately saw trouble ahead. A small group of police officers with machine guns stood outside his compartment. One of them waved to them to come closer. Victor walked slowly, with Veronica right behind him. The officer asked Victor something and Veronica told him Victor didn't understand Serbian.

"English?", the officer asked.

"Actually, Nepalese, but yes, I speak English."

"Is this your place?"

"Yes, my bed is that one", Victor said and pointed.

Victor and Veronica could see how the others held on to the old man in the corridor. They had him handcuffed and pointed guns at him. It was quite dark in the corridor, but Victor's eyes could meet the old man's. They were full of energy, in spite of the apparent humiliation. Whatever could be the reason for this, Victor wondered.

"You talk to him?", the officer asked.

"Very little. He went to eat almost immediately after Belgrade."

"Your bag?", the officer said and pointed to Victor's luggage. There was one suitcase and one backpack.

"Open, please."

Victor opened his suitcase and the officer searched through his clothes, toiletries and some books. Then the backpack. The officer poured its contents on the bed. The cameras, more books, notebooks, rolls of film. There was one book there that wasn't his though: the old Serb's history book. The officer looked at him curiously and then slowly picked up the book. He flipped through the pages and suddenly found a photograph of Victor in there. He held it up to look at.

"Aha. Your book?"

Victor nodded without really knowing why. The officer now put everything back inside the backpack, and asked to see Victor's passport. He wrote down the name and the passport number.

"Nepal? You don't look Nepal."

"I know. It's a strange world."

"And you?", he said and pointed at Veronica.

She answered in Macedonian and he seemed to understand her well. She pointed towards where her compartment was.

"What happened?", Victor asked.

"Very criminal man", the officer said. "Very criminal. OK, thank you. OK now."

Just as Victor and Veronica had locked the compartment door behind them, they could hear some loud commotion in the corridor.

"I hope they treat him OK", Victor whispered. "He seemed like a nice guy to me."

Suddenly there was a loud knock on their door. Had they heard him say that? Veronica opened. The Serbian man was right there, surrounded by the policemen. The man spoke to Veronica.

"He says he has your pen", she said.

One of the police officers handed a fountain pen to Victor.

"It's yours, no?"

Victor nodded and looked at the old man while putting the pen in his breast pocket.

"Thank you", the old man said in broken English. "Good luck with your writing."

The police shut the door and Veronica locked it again. She looked at Victor in amazement.

"What the hell was that about?", she whispered. "Don't tell me you know the guy."

"I don't. Trust me. I have no idea who he is."

"Then why was his book in your backpack?", she asked, while listening close to the door to make sure everyone had moved on.

"How did you know it was his book?", Victor asked her.

"What?! Are you getting paranoid? It's a book in Serbian, Einstein."

"OK. Sure, he must have put it there."

"Please explain to me why there was a photo of you in his book. And why he gave you his pen. That pen wasn't really yours, was it? Is it?"

Victor was tired, a little drunk and in minor shock. He realized he wasn't in any state to figure anything out right now. They were safe and that's what mattered. And they were alone. And horny. At least, he was horny.

"Listen, Veronica. I made a wish that we could spend the night together. Now it seems it is happening. How or why it's happening, I have no idea. But I'm very happy about it. And, when all's said and done, happiness is the only thing that really counts."

They kissed and he unbuttoned her dress for the second time that evening. Soon, all he could hear were her moans. But inside his own mind, her voice was still asking those questions. It was too much, too soon, and especially now that they both rolled over and Veronica straddled him.

17

Shortly before arriving at Skopje in the morning, Victor re-addressed what was usually his main question in life: what the hell was going on? He looked at Veronica, who was radiant and pleasing in every way. He had awoken in love and it was obvious to him that she had too.

When Veronica went to re-join her aunt just before the train arrived at the station, Victor brought out the Serbian book, which was all in Cyrillic typesetting. Veronica would have to translate. He noticed that there was a lot of underlining, which intrigued him. But the weirdest thing was of course his own photograph inside the book. He recognized it. It was taken during a tour of Germany with his band at the time, Blaxpots. This was a long time ago, when Victor had been considerably slimmer.

On the backside of the photograph was written his name, "Victor Ritterstadt". It was absolutely no mistake. The Serb had been there to watch him or follow him or, who knows, hurt him. But the incident with the pen was surely an act of friendship of some strange kind? And the book itself? Victor knew there was always an explanation to everything. The frustrating thing, like now, was not having access to it.

On the platform in Skopje, Veronica finally introduced him to her aunt. She wrote down her telephone number and that was that. Not even a kiss.

He strolled for half an hour with his luggage, taking in the new environment until he found a hotel that seemed nice and fairly central. He had some breakfast sent up, shaved, showered and then ate. On the table lay the Serb's old fountain pen. It was very beautiful, in greenish mother of pearl. A monogram was inscribed in faded gold letters: "E.H." Victor touched it gently and the tried it on a piece of paper. It worked wonderfully well. He took it apart. No secrets inside. He put it together and then wrote his name on the paper. It was nice to write with.

"Good luck with the writing", the man had said. Victor thanked him and the universe for this talismanic gift – for that was surely what it was? Somehow the pen was an amicable sign. The man had had a mission concerning Victor, that much was obvious. It certainly made Victor feel better that the man had been some kind of friend. Or perhaps the Serb had been intercepted by destiny in the shape of Serbian police officers before he could hurt or even kill Victor?

He looked at his watch. 10 a.m. That meant 4 a.m. in New

York. He decided to try and contact his mother again, even though they hadn't agreed on it. He didn't want to call her on the telephone as she might be asleep. Better to say Hi in a dream. Victor decided to see if she was up for some dream time telepathy.

18

Victor sat cross-legged on the floor by his bed after having closed the window and pulled the curtains. The room was now agreeably dim and quiet. He relaxed in body and mind and gradually started visualizing his mother. As he didn't know what she looked like these days, her image was more of an emotional composite, interwoven with words and sentences from their previous communications.

"Mother...", Victor whispered. "I'm here now... Are you around?"

Victor felt very focused and enthusiastic. He kept repeating the same question before his mental picture of her.

On the other side of the Atlantic Ocean, Mary was dreaming vividly. Again, she was a high-flying bird, lightly gliding across the skies. There was a poem that could be heard inside her mind:

"Mary, Mary, mother Mary
Join me now in spheres of light
Mary, Mary, mother Mary
In between the day and night"

Mary allowed herself to return to a hypnagogue state but was careful not to wake up entirely.

"Are you there?", Victor asked.

"Yes, I am", she replied. "Is this a transmission? Are you sending to me?"

"That's an idiotic question, Mom. Anyway, how are you?"

"Great. Better than in a long time actually. I've decided to go back to Nepal. Have you thought about it?"

"Not now, maybe later. I think I want to go. Not sure."

"So how are you?", Mary continued in a perfect state of mind, completely at hypnagogue ease.

"OK. I'm traveling. Meeting people. Amazed. Everything's connected."

19

Suddenly there was a buzz at the Telelabs office in Berlin. A new alarm system had been installed that very same day (at a cost of 30.000 Euro), to really make any personnel aware that there was new activity. Ilse Grokmann stared at her screen, as did Professor Schopenbaur.

"Match it with a map!", he screamed. "Hurry!"

Grokmann oriented herself inside the computer and made what was called a "TAG" (Telepathy Analysis, Geopolitical). As the signals were strong this time, the data were all clear: one point was in or just outside New York City and the other one in Skopje, Macedonia, Europe.

"Keep tracking, keep recording", Schopenbaur said anxiously. "Apply interpretation".

Grokmann labored intensely and she found it exciting. It was obvious that their Berlin source had move a bit. The sending and receiving patterns were exactly the same, only clearer. In her mind, this was due to less mobile phone communications in Skopje than in Berlin.

"Getting there", she whispered.

"Try English", Schopenbaur stammered, excited about the apparent progress and especially pleased that Agent Schwarzenberg was right there behind them, watching their professional attempts at mapping the movements of this potentially dangerous person.

Suddenly some kind of artificial robot voice was heard, like one from a 1950s science-fiction film.

"Record, record!", Schopenbaur screamed.

"Mother... I think I'm in love...", the voice said slowly.

Grokmann and Schopenbaur screamed with joy and spontaneously embraced each other. This was the first time ever they'd been able to actually hear telepathic communications through digital voice-synthesizing.

"I'm happy... Love rules... Love conquers everything...", the voice said.

"Love?", Schwarzenberg said loudly. "Is that some kind of fucking code? Scramble it! Conquer what?"

Professor Schopenbaur couldn't be bothered by the slightly paranoid agent. He just monitored what was going on, as did Grokmann.

"We'll see... She's nice..."

"Very happy to hear it", a different voice said. "I feel I am going back to sleep now. We have to practice more."

"OK. Sleep well. We'll talk more about Nepal soon too. We might want to do that by telephone to get the details right. To a certain extent, certainty can't be applied to this. You've noticed, I think, how our thoughts merge at some point. It's too vague and too subjective an experience. Immersed in immersion, on a path to the undefined giving, taking, change, static, ecstatic, there, here, now... We're going to have to try hard to make something out of both nothing and something else here. We're only parts, Mom, only parts. I think you're doing a great job with the telepathy, by the way. It isn't that hard, is it?"

"Not at all. Good night now."

"Yes. And good morning too."

Telelabs HQ looked at all the data, enthusiastic as children at Christmas time.

"The synthesizer worked so well", Schopenbaur said. "I knew it. Well done, Grokmann. Any news on the locations?"

"A is outside New York, B, who is the main and strongest sender, is in central Skopje in Macedonia. I can't be more precise than that, I'm afraid."

"So was that some kind of code?", Schwarzenberg asked. "They're only parts... Parts of what? And what about Nepal?"

"I don't know", Grokmann answered. "But it was the first time ever that we've been able to hear and record telepathic communications like this. Whoever these people are, they are remarkable. And so, if I may say so, are we."

20

In various secret locations in and around Berlin, several people looked at their own colleagues, stunned by what they had just heard in this highly monitored Telelabs frenzy. Regardless of their nationality and their views on the ownership of production-lines and their own sub rosa self interests, the message was exactly the same: get to Skopje and isolate the main sender before anyone else does.

21

After having rested for a while, Victor called Veronica. She was at home and they agreed to meet later in the afternoon. Victor looked out the window. He knew right away that he loved this town. Although the main square was ugly and modern in the worst possible sense, he could see that it was still surrounded by the beauty of old age, of history. He loved traveling in Eastern Europe and this was one good reason why: there was still some kind of genuine human soul around.

He decided to go on a short camera stroll to clear his mind. The receptionist recommended Macedonia Street, which was right outside. He walked and walked and watched and watched. The desire to take pictures wasn't really present though. Perhaps I don't need to document absolutely everything all the time, he thought.

After walking the street up and down several times, he sat down to rest at a sidewalk café. People were drifting in every direction. A small group of people were watching some clowns who were fooling around and panhandling. One of them was on top of a really old bicycle, the kind of model that had an absurdly large front wheel. It looked dangerous but the clown was obviously in control of things (although he did wobble a lot) and made people laugh. Victor laughed too, as he wondered how anyone could ever envision or construct a vehicle like that.

Victor took some photos of the spectacle from his table. He could also see some young boys trying to pick-pocket their way through the crowd, and he got distanced photos of everything. It amused him. The boys weren't all that successful. The locals knew exactly where the boys were and if they got too close, they were either stared down or pushed away.

22

When Veronica knocked on his door, he had more or less just returned from his stroll. They were happy to see each other and without wasting any time whatsoever made love again. It was as if they wanted to check if their dream was still a dream. It certainly seemed to be that way, and as they got dressed again, all they could really express was a shared and satisfied smile.

"Are we eating out?", Victor asked her.

"Of course. What would you like to eat?"

"I'm hungry as hell actually. You know, I've had some incredible meals in both Croatia and Serbia. Meat-memories, wonderful meat-memories. Do you think Skopje can beat them?"

"Of course", Veronica said. "We'll go to the Old Bazaar and have a meal there. The meat meal of all meat meals."

It was early evening when they entered a zone apparently forgotten by time. The old Turkish part of Skopje, now predominantly populated by Albanians, was a colorful maze of narrow alleys and small shops filled with everything from Chinese plastic toys to real antiques. Victor felt at home here: yet another space and time supremely reigned by in betweenness.

They found a restaurant and sat down by the window. Victor looked at Veronica in the soft light that was filtered through thin, white curtains. She was beautiful, witty and full of stories about Skopje and this part of town. She called it a magical place. The entire setting was indeed magical to Victor. Yet he couldn't stop thinking about the Serb and his book. He mentioned this to Veronica, who agreed it was a completely mind-boggling mystery.

"I thought I recognized him somehow", she said. "I don't know, but when I was a girl there was a kind of health prophet around, in magazines and on TV all over Yugoslavia. You know, talking about hiking, bicycling, mountaineering. Not sports like in the Olympics but just basically trying to get people out into nature. He reminded me of that guy. He seemed just as... Alive."

"I hope he still is", Victor said. "He didn't seem like a criminal to me."

"Who knows? If you want me to, I could look at his book later on. But tonight is fun night, OK?"

"Sure. I actually have the book with me. But we can wait.

What's your idea of fun, then?"

"To be with you and make sure you have fun."

"But what if I don't know how to have fun?"

"Then I'll have to teach you."

They laughed loudly as the waiter brought them their menus. The sun pierced some heavy, grey clouds and Skopje became a little bit more colorful again.

Later in the evening they strolled through the bazaar. Most of the shops were open late. Victor bought Veronica a Chinese incense-holder and a big Chinese soapstone for himself. It was heavy and cumbersome but he knew he had to have it. It reminded him of jade, but also of the Serbian man's fountain pen.

Back at the hotel, the night receptionist greeted them nervously. Victor thought it was just because he was bringing a Macedonian woman up to his room. Victor couldn't really see how that could be a problem though. When they reached the door to his room, they noticed it was slightly open. Victor pushed it open. There was no one in there but he was sure that someone had been there, and that recently.

"Are you sure?", Veronica whispered.

"Absolutely. The suitcase is open. I left it closed. Someone's been here."

He poured all of his clothes on the bed, with some books that were also in the suitcase. Nothing seemed to be missing, not even the books he'd brought for the trip. All the other hard stuff – cameras, film, his journal – was in the backpack on his back. Including the Serb's book. Victor was certain this little visit had something to do with their brief encounter the night before.

"Are you afraid?", Veronica asked.

"Not a bit. In a weird way, I feel almost honored. Whatever is going on must be important. And you?"

"To tell you the truth, I feel a little bit excited", she said and smiled.

"OK", Victor said and locked the door. "I can handle that too."

Within seconds, they were passionately united again. Veronica lay underneath him, receiving each thrust with a high-pitched moan. Victor hadn't enjoyed sex this much in a long time and it certainly empowered him to the extent that he wasn't merely going to use it for gratuitous sensuality.

He slowed down the pace and started fucking her deeper and more rhythmically instead. As they kissed, Victor used the sexual energy to open up vistas of his mind, the goal being inquisitive. As Veronica felt so nice to be inside, he had a hard time focusing, but he did. He could see the nervous hotel receptionist's eyes looking to the left and to the right but nothing was to be seen. Then some white vans parked close to the hotel. Then an image of himself, sticking his head into his own backpack. That was it. He couldn't resist the temptation anymore. Veronica clung to him and pressed herself against him tightly. He came inside her and had spontaneous visions of clowns on 19th century bicycles.

"Will you stay the night?", Victor asked her when they'd calmed down again.

"If you want me to", she said and kissed him.

"I do."

Victor went to the window. He could indeed see a white van parked nearby. Had he seen it as they were on their way in or had his inner vision been correct? He decided it didn't really matter.

"We stay, we sleep, but tomorrow I will definitely check out from this place."

"I have an idea", Veronica said. "My aunt and uncle have a house in the countryside. It's very nice. I mean, you haven't really seen much of Skopje but the countryside is lovely and we could always return later."

"It sounds fantastic. Let's do that. Am I keeping you from something by the way? Work, studying?"

"Nothing that can't wait", she said and smiled. "I want to help you. I really do."

23

They slept well and heavily, entangled in each other's sweaty limbs. Victor woke early and got up to shower and think. At eight a.m. they were down in the lobby to check out. The receptionist was still on his shift.

"Checking out?", he asked.

"Yes, very much so", Victor replied.

"I hope your stay was good."

"Indeed it was. Best I've had today."

The young man looked slightly confused but decided it was best left alone. Especially as he could now see Victor outside, taking pictures of the white van. After all, it was someone from that very van who had so graciously provided him with a generous tip last evening, in exchange for his master key a short while.

"Is anyone inside?", Veronica asked.

"If they are, they're probably in the back. I'm just going to leave a message."

He affixed a piece of paper to one of the windshield wipers and then left together with his Macedonian maiden in the direction of the old bazaar again. If they were being followed that would be the best place to lose someone. They looked back from time to time but no one suspicious could be seen. They could even see the white van in the distance, still parked in front of the hotel.

What they hadn't seen was how the receptionist had gone out to remove the piece of paper from the van's front window. He looked at it and made a call from his mobile phone.

"Yes, it's me. The front desk. You wanted me to call. He checked out just now. He left a paper on the car. Yes, handwritten. OK, it's like this..."

"To whom it may concern,

The rectal fibers of the universe, displaying themselves through anticipated shortcomings. If there were gateways, they would be gateways into the intestines of a being or a becoming of age. An age of reason and consent before it's too late. The deeper we claim to penetrate the so called mysteries, the more we have to realize that the effort is in vain. What mysteries can be found in the intestines of the unknown? Some would say "Nothing" and some would say "All the substance there ever was". What appears colorful and enticing to some, is irrevocably disgusting to others. All mysteries remain mysteries. It's in their nature. All natures remain natural. It's in their mystery. A mystery displaying itself through and as an age of consent.

Sincerely, Victor Ritterstadt

P.S. If you ever want to find me, just go fuck yourself, because that's where I'll be."

"That was it", the receptionist said. "I know. Very strange. No, nothing more. OK, good-bye."

24

A couple of days later, Victor and Veronica were settled in a cottage near the Matka Canyon. Veronica had arranged everything and had even borrowed a car from some relatives. Victor was truly amazed at how this young woman had become so devoted to his wellbeing in basically no time at all.

The scenery at Matka was breathtaking. There was a river close by, mighty and slow-moving through a high cliff landscape. They could take care of their own household and there were also several villages nearby if they needed anything. Victor's first impulse was not to have more sex or go hiking, as he'd expected. First of all, he wanted to start writing. This was a serene place to write and in many ways the cliffs and mountains reminded him of his beloved Nepalese Himalayas. High and rocky, yet lush and full of chlorophyllic saturation.

On their first evening in the cottage, Victor and Veronica had looked at the Serbian book. She said it was an ordinary book about the history of science. There was a great deal of underlining and she translated these sections for Victor. He listened attentively but still couldn't make any logical ends meet properly.

In one section on the Serbian inventor Nikola Tesla, Veronica found a marginal note saying "NB, VR, NB". The ordinary interpretation of "NB" would be "Nota Bene", as in "Please note". And "VR" could well be his own initials. "Please note, Victor Ritterstadt, please note!" Or was this too far-fetched?

This section, that was also entirely underlined, was about Tesla's initial experiments with air-based distribution of electricity, from one generator to a receiving station. Victor had heard about this, and about Tesla, but nothing really substantial. He did find it highly interesting though. OK, so the old Serb had wanted to point this out to Victor. But why?

"Perhaps he knew he was getting caught and wanted to talk to you before this?", Veronica suggested.

"Sure, but why? To hand over this book? It sounds a little bit too much. Or too little."

"Maybe. But the photo means he really was after you. And the pen is surely a symbol of trust, a torch, a gift that empowers?"

"Wow, you're good, Veronica", he said. "You really are. I agree completely. But, again, why me?"

"Look, there's something weird here. See, take a look at this page."

Veronica held the page in question under the lamp. They could both clearly see a faint underlining of the letter "m" in one sentence.

"Is there more? Let's check from the beginning."

They sat down close together and opened the Tesla chapter at the beginning. Page after page was thoroughly scrutinized. And they did indeed find something: more underlined letters. At first, "w", "w" and "w", indicating an Internet address. This continued to make sense, as the ensuing letters spelled out the specific name of an Internet file transfer site.

"This is scary", Veronica said.

"Oh yeah? Whatever happened to the excitement?"

They wrote down the entire address. It was without a doubt a web site address. There wasn't any computer in the cottage so they'd have to wait until the next day. If they couldn't find one close by, they could go back to Skopje and find out more there.

25

To be on the safe side, they did go back to Skopje the following morning, where Victor bought a laptop computer, a mobile Internet connection, a small printer and printer paper. He set the computer up in the car while Veronica was driving back to Matka again, and everything seemed to be working. There was battery power to get started with, at least.

He entered the web site address they had written down. A minimalist page with the text "Please check connection. This file can only be downloaded once." He told Veronica to stop somewhere soon, as the connection seemed pretty good there. It probably wouldn't be out in the Macedonian countryside. Veronica pulled over at a gas station with a small kiosk and bistro attached.

Parked safely, Victor looked at her.

"Yes, there's a file here alright. I'm going to download it."

"Do it", she answered.

Victor did. They both followed the progress bar on the screen that moved slowly and in jerks. The connection seemed OK, so why was it moving so slowly?

Suddenly there was a knock on the car window. They both jumped in their seats. A smiling toothless man outside asked loudly if they wanted their windows wiped. Veronica answered him equally loudly and the man walked away, still smiling. Their attention returned to the computer screen. Almost done, almost downloaded. When the download process was completed, Victor checked to see that the file was on the computer desktop, then shut it down and told Veronica to move on.

"We'll look at it later... Now it's there... It's a simple PDF file, so we'll be able to open it later."

"Okeydokey... That guy really scared me", Veronica answered and started the car. She looked at the man in the rear view mirror, who was now talking to two other men, all looking at her and smiling.

26

Back in the cottage at Matka, they were both anxious to see what the fuss was all about. Victor set up the computer, turned it on and sat down by the table. He opened the file. It was based of almost a hundred pages with detailed descriptions and old plans and sketches for what seemed to be an exercise bicycle. Victor was a bit puzzled. Veronica looked over each page and translated bits for him while still reading.

"So what is it? What's the mystery?", he asked her.

"It's an electrical generator connected to a bike", she answered.

"Oh? You mean like for a bicycle lamp? But that already exists...", Victor replied.

"This seems to be something else. It seems to generate more power than for a tiny lamp. I don't know. It comes from Tesla or someone who worked with him. But there's not only that.

There's also something about transmitting this electricity in the air, from one generator to a receiving station. I'm sorry, I don't understand."

"Don't worry about it...", Victor told her. "We have done what we could. The guy obviously wanted me to have this. Why? I'm sure we'll find out at some point."

"I am too. It says here that a connected network of 1000 bicycles that are used one hour daily could provide a city the size of Belgrade with all the electricity it needs."

"Oh dear, then it really is like I suspected", Victor sighed.

"Meaning what?"

"That this is something that people will be willing to kill for. Governments, companies, gangs... Either to stow away or to exploit..."

"But maybe this is known already", Veronica suggested.

"Maybe... But why would someone go through the effort to get me this file if it's already available somewhere?"

"I'm a little bit scared...", Veronica said and hugged Victor.

"To tell you the truth, so am I. But remember always, Veronica, that basically all we can and have to do is just to do what we have to do. Am I making myself clear?"

"Crystal clear, my dear", Veronica said and started unbuttoning Victor's shirt.

27

Mary tried connecting with her son telepathically from time to time but failed. It wasn't that it didn't work, but rather that Victor was preoccupied with other things. He and Veronica strolled through the majestic autumn landscape at Matka, explored caves, took photos. They ate simple food, drank wine, made love and enjoyed life.

"Tomorrow, let's go to Vrelo", Veronica suggested.

"Absolutely. What is it?"

"It's a big cave. An underwater cave. Very strange place. I want to take you there."

28

It was a beautiful and sunny day as they rowed down the Treska river in a small boat they had borrowed from some neighbors, looking up at the steep green hillsides. Victor looked forward to seeing this. It didn't take long before they reached the opening of the Vrelo. The cave was big and the river made small lakes in there. Stalactites created an eerie atmosphere, which was welcoming and frightening at the same time.

"Wow, it feels just like being inside a womb...", Victor whispered.

"That's right", Veronica replied. "Matka means womb, by the way. People often come in here to do magic. This is where everything begins. That's why I've brought you here. You can make a wish here. You should make a wish here. Let me hear it. Let the cave hear it."

Victor looked at her. In the subdued light of the cave, Veronica now looked like some unearthly creature. She was no longer a young Macedonian woman set on having a good time. She was now something completely different, an ageless, archetypical witch of some sort. Victor closed his eyes.

"I wish for health, wealth and length of days", he began. "And a safe and successful development of this electricity project. And a girlfriend who sees my needs and heeds them. A girlfriend who doesn't feel the need to compete with me on an intellectual level. Someone who respects my creativity. I don't need stimulation on an intellectual level from a girlfriend. From her, I need emotional tenderness, caring, sex, a fulfilment of all those things I can't arrange myself, on my own. Beauty, esprit, allure, tenderness, love, self sacrifice, an intelligent Florence Nightingale rather than just another neurotic artist like myself.

I wish for international culture, ego gratification, reaching out while reaching in. To manifestly become what I already am on the inside: an intelligent and cultured artist with the power and poetry to enrich others' lives. One who inspires to celebrate life and its possibilities more. Not shying away from the dark aspects, but not striving for a constructed darkness either. Writing freely, experimenting and seeing what comes. And valuing the process highly. Gently jerking always brings something. That which comes, those who come – an extrapolation of phallic energy and fertile seed in a different and less sticky and perhaps less offensive form. Protagonist seed-sowing. I wish for action rather than far too modest reaction.

I wish that every moment should be filled by the holy guardian angel, the healing gordian angle, the main inspiration, the daimon, the hidden genius. In invocation, and in evocation through me. The evocation is the work process and its results, while the invocation is the awareness, the increased consciousness of what's going on. Not at all rationally, hampering the synchronicities and the twists of inspiration and creativity. But joyfully and with an open mind. Editing may be done. But editing can't come before the creation. That's the number one: creation. That is, writing. Everything else is but different fruits on the same tree.

By all means, I should continue to listen to the spirits, mentors, inspirations. Listening by reading and assimilating what's uniquely them. What can I learn? How can I learn? But I should listen even more closely to my own voice and my own spirit. The expression, content, form and style must be mine and mine alone.

I wish that criticism need not concern me. I have my voice and it will speak its own mind in its own way. Jealousy and hostile tendencies from others have nothing to do with me. I have my voice and it needs to speak. Be shameless about it, if need be. Talismanic teachings and cathartic correspondence. If others aren't interested or perhaps even actively disinterested, then so be it.

I wish for all of these things but am happy for only a fraction of it all. Many thanks. Many thanks, Matka. Many thanks, Veronica. Many thanks, Vrelo womb."

Victor opened his eyes again. Veronica smiled. He rowed the boat out into the open air again. He felt completely phased and a little bit drained of energy.

"You don't have to say anything", Veronica said, understanding the awe perfectly. "And you did say quite a great deal in there."

"Was it too much?", he asked.

"For some people, you're probably too much. For me, you're just perfect. You want a lot and can express it. I'm really envious of that. From now on I'm going to practice on that. Not in order to become you, but in order to become me."

"Sounds perfect. Where to next, my dear?"

"Keep rowing", Veronica said and laughed. "There are more caves up ahead."

29

Back at their cottage later in the evening, Victor knew that sooner or later he'd have to break up their little paradise at Matka. But it didn't necessarily have to be without Veronica at all.

"I have to leave soon. I'm going to Nepal. Do you want to come along?", he asked her.

"Not right now, no...", Veronica answered. "I have a job that I need to do, you know the teacher thing. I took some time off to go with you here, but soon I have to go back."

"I'll miss you", Victor said and kissed her.

"I'll miss you too. But there's always the future, right?"

"Yes. There's always the future. I'm sad to say I have to get back to Berlin pretty soon, and then leave from there."

"Don't be sad. You're in an amazing adventure. I'm the one who should be sad."

"Don't be sad", Victor replied. "You're in an amazing adventure too. None of us should be sad. Let's just move onwards. Who knows, you know, what seems to be different directions might just be parallel again after a while."

"I'm sure you say that to all the girls you meet. It's almost as cheap as saying that I'm 'number one' or something like that...", Veronica said.

"Perhaps, darling, but I only mean it when I say it to you..."

They both burst out laughing, happy and sad at the same time.

"What are you doing with the document?", Veronica continued.

"I'll hang on to that. But I'm giving you a printed copy of it."

"Why?", she asked.

"As a back up. As a sign of trust. As a sign that we've shared something mysterious."

"But what if I sell it to some evil power corporation that just exploits it or, worse, stashes it away while making billions off the very last drops of oil?"

"Then that's how it is and that's how it was", Victor replied. "I think you'll be a good girl about it though. I think you'll hang on to it and await further orders. Just keep it safe and don't tell anyone you have it. The adventure will continue, you know, sooner or later."

"I know that", Veronica replied and smiled. "I know that."

30

As Mary passed through the Nepalese passport control, the officer looked at her strangely. She was sure this man was used to old hippies coming back, either to relive old memories or to go trekking in the mountains. Mary intended to do both, but of course most of all to resume where she left off, as a mother goddess to a somewhat secret love cult. Mary smiled at him. He smiled back. Then he looked at a Western-looking plainclothes-man. This man looked very serious, suddenly stood up and signaled Mary over.

"Madame, please come in here", he said and led her into a small cubicle.

"Is something wrong?", Mary asked.

"On the contrary. Welcome to Nepal", he said silently.

"Thank you", she replied. "Are you American?"

He nodded. Mary didn't dare ask what he was doing there. Or what she was doing there with him.

"Listen, I know who you are. I'm with you. It's an honor to meet you. You should have this. It's my card. If you ever need anything, just call me. I live here, in Thamel, in Kathmandu. When I was younger, I was up there... You know, in the village."

Mary couldn't understand if he was just very friendly or some kind of government spy. She felt dizzy.

"Oh, have we met before, you mean?", Mary asked him.

"Unfortunately not. I was there later, after you'd left. But I was immersed in the story and I believe in it. That's why it's an honor to greet you here. Please be aware that there are many people who are interested in what you and your son are up to. You're safe up there where you're going. But please be careful."

"What? What do you mean?", Mary whispered.

"It doesn't matter right now. I'm a friend. Please trust me. Let me know if you need anything. Remember, you can call me anytime, Mary. OK, you're done here. Have a nice time in Nepal."

Mary left the airport terminal, more confused than ever before. As soon as she was out of sight, the man sat down by a telephone and dialed.

"Get me Rover, please. Yes, I know very well there's no one there by that name, but please connect me anyway. Thanks. OK... Sir? Yes, it's me. She just passed through. She seems, well, totally harmless. But we can never know for sure with these people. Are you sure she's that guy's mother? Because if not, I have really goofed. Alright. OK, thank you very much. Bye."

31

Victor returned to Berlin late on a Friday night. It was drizzling, grey and cold, a stark contrast to sunny Macedonia. He took a taxi from the airport to the apartment close to Bahnhof Zoo. He rented two rooms from a Frau Nowak, who had inherited a grand but run down ten room apartment from her husband. It was far too big for her alone, so she sublet all that she could. Currently there were only Victor and Otto, an unsuccessful young musician of sorts. He often knocked on Victor's door to play him a new song or two. Victor found the material dreadfully dull, but kept a straight face out of sheer politeness.

"What? Why?", Otto asked when Victor told him and Frau Nowak of his plans over a cup of late night tea.

"I need to be on my way, simple as that", Victor replied.

"That's a shame. I have enjoyed your company", Frau Nowak admitted, making sure Otto would notice her smile. "Please don't forget that you'll have to pay next month's rent too, as agreed."

"Not a problem, Frau Nowak", Victor answered.

"What exactly is it that you're going to do?", Otto continued.

"I'm going to trek in the Himalayas", Victor said, not straying too far from the truth.

"Ugh! Some kind of Zarathustra trip? That's so bourgeois,

Victor", Otto said.

"Well, there you go. That's me in a nutshell: a bourgeois Zarathustra."

"Hey come on Victor, that's a paradox and you know it."

"Exactly", Victor replied.

"Exactly what?"

"It's a paradox and I know it."

"I see. You're in your cosmic mood again. Well OK then, safe journeys, you amateur Zarathustra!"

"Come on, Otto, leave him be. And speaking of bourgeois things, it's time for you to pay your rent too", Frau Nowak said.

Victor excused himself and went into his bedroom. Being back, he missed Veronica and her wit but knew that the feeling would calm down eventually. Or would it?

32

The following days were hard work. Otto helped Victor haul boxes of books and personal belongings into a self storage warehouse. He was only going to bring the essential cameras, notebooks, the laptop computer he'd bought in Macedonia and a basic set of clothes. After this, securing the flight tickets, paying some final bills and Frau Nowak and also providing Otto with some cash. As much as he disliked the one-directional flow of pecuniary energy, Victor felt genuinely sorry for Otto and hoped he could get up on his own two feet somehow. Giving him some petty cash probably wouldn't help at all but it was definitely better than nothing. A nice gesture, anyway.

Thinking about Otto brought back memories from Victor's own youth. Being financially independent had always been important to Victor, but whenever he looked back, it was clear to see that his independence had always been heavily subsidized by patrons and benevolent people who supported whatever he was up to at the time. As he'd been moving around in the environs of underground culture, there hadn't been much money there anyway. But Victor was proud that he could now make enough money to get by, simply by working with his art. In his mind, that really was something to be proud of. Berlin had been especially good in that sense, as he'd been able to sell a lot of photographs there.

But now things were changing again, and he was getting ready to embrace his role as guru or magician or whatever it was that the Nepalese were after. Not forgetting the role of long lost son or, rather, son to a long lost mother.

On the eve of his leaving, he took Frau Nowak and Otto out to dinner at his favorite Berlin restaurant, the Paris Bar. It was nice enough and everyone was happy. Victor was more anxious to try and contact his mother again though. If he had understood everything correctly, she would now actually be in Nepal. While chatting away with his landlady and the disgruntled Otto, one section of his mind tried to tune in to telepathy, asking if Mary was around. But no such luck. Too much going on in left brain hemispheres and too much human noise around them.

33

Ilse Grokmann noticed a slight tremor in her equipment and could clearly see that it was the same frequency as usual. And that it was close by, not in Macedonia. Really close by. She called her superior, as instructed.

"And you're saying this is in central Berlin?"

"Yes, close to Bahnhof Zoo", Grokmann replied.

"Damn. How could he have escaped us? Let me know if anything changes, OK? We'll be right over."

"OK. See you soon."

Ilse Grokmann sighed. These people were total cretins. She was interested in telepathy research, not in being involved with idiots. She was sure she could get more results on her own. The problem was that she didn't share her colleagues' desire to track down and interrogate. It was so obvious that they were dealing with an advanced spiritual human being. Or possibly someone with a cerebral disorder that allowed for this kind of extrasensory communication. But how did people like that find each other? Ilse was certain that she could learn more by being friendly to a person like that. Or persons.

Ilse's gear was silent. She was alone. She closed her eyes and tried to calm down, breathing slowly. She remembered the telepathic conversations they'd overheard at Telelabs. She tried to resonate with the Berlin sender without really knowing how. A strange kind of silence. She was used to meditating and allowed herself to sink a little deeper into herself. Mentally, silently, slowly she called for the man in Berlin, over and over. She floated away in her relaxation and focused on the mantra-like calling.

34

At the Paris Bar, Victor was startled by a strange voice inside his head. At first, he thought it was Mary, but it was just too different. He accidentally knocked over his glass of beer right down on Otto's lap.

"I'm so sorry...", Victor said.

Otto, stood up, his pants soaked with beer. People around them laughed. A waiter hurried to the table and wiped up he liquid while Otto went to the rest room. Inside Victor's head was someone asking to see the man in Berlin. He needed to focus. Frau Nowak looked at him, wondering if everything was OK.

"I'm here in Berlin. Who wants to know?", Victor transmitted silently.

"A friend. I'm a friend."

Ilse's monitor lit up and the recording device, which was set on auto record, started. But the proximity of Ilse's own transmission to the equipment created a telepathy feedback loop which was louder than anything she'd ever heard before. Ilse threw off her headphones, screamed and ran out of the room.

At Victor's table, there was inner silence again. Although Otto loudly insisted on another beer, they all decided to go home instead. While walking back, Victor realized that someone must have tried to contact him and him alone. Whether friend or foe he couldn't really tell. But it was certainly interesting enough that this occurred on the night before his leaving for Asia.

35

No one had noticed Ilse Grokmann's erratic behavior, and for that she was very grateful. She calmed down, went to the Telelabs rest room, splashed some cold water in her face and then returned to her desk. At the same time, Schopenbaur and agent Schwarzenberg returned.

"We have news, Ilse", Schopenbaur said. "Our man is here in Berlin right now."

Grokmann looked at him. What was he talking about? She had told him that already half an hour ago.

"If it really is who we suspect it is, he's booked on a flight to Bangkok tomorrow."

"How nice for him", Grokmann replied.

"And for you, Ilse. You're going too."

Grokmann rose from her chair with a surprised expression on her face.

"You heard me", Schopenbaur said. "The other field agents are... Well, they're still in Macedonia. All you have to do is keep an eye on him and report."

"Nothing else?", Grokmann wondered, already making plans for her own telepathic experiments.

"Keep your distance, Grokmann", Schwarzenberg said. "It's very likely that we're dealing with a highly dangerous person or group here. His name is Victor Ritterstadt. You'll get all the relevant information before you leave tomorrow. We would never send a woman if we didn't have faith in your capacity, Grokmann. He's going to Bangkok, so that very likely means he's involved with drugs and prostitution. Can you handle that, Grokmann?"

"Handle what?"

"Drugs and prostitution."

"Oh, I would never charge for sex", she replied.

"That's not what he means, Ilse dear", Schopenbaur said. "He just wants you to be careful. You're booked on the same flight tomorrow. Go home now and pack and call me later."

Schwarzenberg went over to the other side of the room to make a phone call. Schopenbaur pulled Grokmann aside and talked to her quietly.

"Make contact if you can. Try and figure out more. But for

us, not for them. I've been promised more funding if we can find out more, but I only want to feed them small bits. This is official government work now, Ilse, so consider it a paid vacation. If you can find out more, I might give you a raise too. Whatever it takes, in the name of science! Understood?"

"Understood, Sir!", Grokmann replied. "Whatever it takes, in the name of science!"

Leaving the building, it struck her that her own desire of only ten minutes ago – that of handling this research entirely on her own – was now on its way to manifest. There was apparently more to telepathy, and to Victor Ritterstadt, than she had ever expected. She just had to make sure to avoid those strange telepathy feedback loops.

36

As the plane had left the ground and the Fasten Seatbelt-sign had been switched off, Victor stretched his legs and went to the tiny rest room. He preferred to sleep on long flights so he might as well have a meal and then try to sleep as much as possible.

When he returned, his neighbor stretched out a hand to greet him.

"Hello, I'm Ilse", she said.

"Hello, I'm Victor."

"You're on your way to Bangkok?"

"Well, that's where this plane is going", Victor replied.

They both laughed as he sat down again. She apparently wanted to talk a bit. Perhaps she was nervous or something. I'll give her a while and then explain that it's bedtime for me, Victor thought.

"What do you do?", Ilse asked.

"Art, I deal with art", Victor replied.

"Oh, that sounds like it's profitable."

"Not really. I deal with art, not in art. I'm an artist, not a dealer. I mean, I deal with it everyday, but I don't deal in it."

"Oh, I see... That sounds interesting. I deal with the human mind myself. Psychology, parapsychology, communication...", Grokmann continued and looked straight at him.

Victor immediately became suspicious. The Paris Bar intermezzo on the evening before and now someone here right next to him willingly talking to a stranger of very strange things.

"Oh, that sounds interesting too", Victor began. "Are you dealing with your own mind or that of others?"

"Mine isn't very interesting, I'm afraid. I try to learn from others, from other people's minds."

"I see, like some kind of mind reading?", Victor asked.

"Ah, I wouldn't go so far perhaps", Grokmann replied. "But of course there are always new things to discover. I'm a scientist first and foremost. Other people's experiences interest me."

Victor looked the woman deep in her eyes. He didn't like her. Not at all. Whatever her real interest was, it was no coincidence that she was there beside him. He didn't quite understand why or how, but she was bad news. He kept looking her in the eyes.

"And what about hypnosis?", he asked her quietly, almost intimately.

"What about it? Why are you looking at me like that?"

"Does it also interest you?"

"I... don't... know... I... don't... believe...", she replied.

"Oh, you don't have to believe in anything, Ilse. That's the beauty of it. But you are feeling very tired now, aren't you? You are feeling very, very, very tired now, aren't you?"

Grokmann unwillingly closed her eyes and suddenly slumped in her chair. When Victor had checked that she was truly fast asleep, he got out the black blinds from the night time courtesy package and put them over her eyes.

37

It was late in the afternoon when Mary heard a car coming in. She knew this was it. Rama had tried to keep it a secret but had failed. Victor was flying into Kathmandu from Bangkok that very same day. Mary went outside, braced herself and watched the car pull up. She could see Rama in there. He got out, followed by someone who Mary knew would have to be Victor.

"Look who we have here", Rama said and smiled as Victor came up to Mary.

"Mommy dearest, I presume?", he said.

Mary couldn't say a word. They hugged. They looked each other over. Mary could feel the tears coming. They hugged again.

"This is my mother, right, Rama?", Victor said to Rama.

They all laughed. People approached them with fresh flowers. There was no chaos, just a serene flocking of people who wanted to touch Victor. Even the Westerners were in awe at their reunion.

"It's been so long. It's been too long", Rama said. "Come, let's get your things inside."

They all agreed not to stress anything. They just sat down in the shade, everyone welcome. They were brought coffee and drinks and just sat looking at each other and around themselves. It was almost the same feeling Mary had originally had when she first came to Nepal in 1970. This was as real as it was back then. She wanted to say that she just couldn't believe it, but didn't. She did believe it now. She did believe life could be this incredible.

"Well, how have you been?", Victor said.

"Shouldn't that be my question?", Mary replied.

"I beat you to it."

"I'm fine. I feel like I'm waking up after a long dream."

"A bad one?"

"More or less. Maybe inexplicable is a better word."

"Tell me about it."

"Well, at first I came back..."

"I meant yes, sure, I understand", Victor laughed.

"Oh. OK. And you?"

He fell silent and smiled at the crowd who sat around them, some doing things and some just hanging out, having a drink and looking at Victor and his mother, shyly.

"Whatever I say usually sounds like some high strung dogmatic platitude", he went on. "But that's just how I am. I have to say it feels good to be here again. I always loved the mountains. They're still here, I'm happy to see. I fought it, I guess. I fought being who I am."

"We all do. At least you had a chance to do your own thing."

"Do my own thing? My, my, you really are an old hippie, aren't you? Basically, what I've been doing for the past twenty years is trying to juggle all the contradicting messages in my own head. Now it seems one side has won and here I am. If this is my own thing, we have yet to see."

"I hope it is. I want to be here with you."

"You are."

"Forever."

"Forever? There is no such thing and you know it. I really don't need any more projections or demands in my life. I accept you as my mother, that we're here now, and that's fair and fine. But please remember that you're also a total stranger to me."

"Let's just go slow then. We have time. I want to get to know you. It seems these people do too. I think you look great, by the way. You seem balanced. Are you happy? Tell me about your work."

"Happy?", he asked. "Who can tell? Other people keep referring to me as an artist and I accept that. I write, I take photos, I make music and occasionally I mix all three ingredients. To be somewhat balanced and alive I need to read, write and think every day. That's what I strive for, to have the designated time to do that every day. If I've managed that, I've thereby created art. Both on the level of manifesting general existential choices and, more literally, of allowing something to be created through those choices. All of these things and levels are interconnected. The writing is the purest channel of transmission for me and very often where I sow seeds that later tend to grow either as visual stimulation or musical structures."

"It seems your seeds are growing and blooming here with us again," Rama said and smiled.

"Over the years I've certainly had my share of internal struggles about this... Right after I left Nepal, I decided to follow my own intuition and later on my own will. This could have been fairly easy had my interest or will been limited to one specific thing, like, for instance, writing. But in my case, it's been a mix of these three things, as you know, Rama. We've talked about this before. These parts have been the essence of my life. Now I just live with that. One good thing about being diligent and hardworking is that as you grow older, there's bound to be, if not fame, then at least infamy. I keep repeating that. Maybe it'll be true one day."

They laughed, and Mary could see he was a bit uneasy at the

expected response. He made a joke, they all laughed. It was pretty predictable. She could tell he'd been giving this some serious thought. Perhaps even a bit too much thought.

"That sounds reasonable enough", Mary said. "I've checked... You've done so much stuff. But haven't you ever felt that you've worked too hard without stopping and checking if people are listening in the first place?"

"You got me there. Of course. It's made me tired. Both the work and to even think about it. Call it a delusion if you want, but that sense of misdirection has been there all along."

"Perhaps you've been preaching unnecessarily to the already converted?"

"Maybe you're right. It's the same pattern all over. In art, in ventures, life, even work with the Order. It's made me tired, I have to say."

"The Order? You mean that occult group? Well, don't you think they had good use for you?"

"I'm sure they did", he replied. "I'd hate to see all that work wasted. I often felt it was completely misdirected. And then, that they spit me out when I wasn't productive anymore. But art just can't be separated from the magical and mythical elements and their deep-rooted connections in the human mind. If that's not there, we're only talking about illustration, decoration or ego-masturbation. But art has a much, much larger potential than that."

"I think you've put in quite enough", Mary said. "Maybe they simply saw that you could stand on your own two feet? Isn't that really what it's all about? Remember the philosophy you were espousing. Finding your will, making sure it comes to fruition. You've done that, haven't you?"

He nodded. They were in agreement. His very human desire to be admired had taken a toll over a long period of time, and his seemingly unlimited capacity for work had apparently very much been used by several people who may not have been malevolent, but just rather street-smart. As his mother, Mary felt a bit sorry for him. On the other hand, he had been a lot more successful than he cared to admit.

"The main dilemma, I think, is that I'm not as obsessed by storytelling as I think I should be", Victor began again. "I don't wake up every morning and just can't wait to start writing. Is it a passion? Shouldn't it be? Or is it simply a matter of self-discipline? As often, I'm stuck in constructions, preconceived notions, the stage magic of words through which I make myself disappear. Concepts that become so ambitious they will never see the manifested light of day. Perhaps an implemented increased self-discipline will help here? I don't lack the talent, of that I'm certain. But where is the goal – if there is one? What are my ambitions, other than those firmly connected in the results? You know, the lifestyle, projections from others, etc?"

"Maybe the goal is just simply to live and then to tell that story?", Mary intercepted.

"You're right, mom. Wow, it feel strange to say that. But you're absolutely right. And from that perspective, I can see that there's a lot to be written about. I feel ashamed that perhaps the only thing I've been missing is... You. To have some kind of stamp of approval. I know it sounds totally pathetic."

"No, it doesn't. Not at all. I feel sorry that I haven't been there for you earlier, to help you with that. Yet you've done so much on your own."

"It's a hard and lonely job", Victor continued. "The loneliness I'm certainly used to and, to be honest, quite comfortable with. But there must be something to write about: stories, fiction, fact, travel, art, etc. I'm disappointed by journalism – or so I claim. But what I suspect I really lack is a structure in which I can work. In which there's an amount of recognition on two main levels: the archetypical editor who sees me and the money I'm paid."

"So what are you going to do? Are you going to stay here and write?"

"Book projects abound", Victor went on. "I have to define them clearer than I have so far. What is the book about and why? Clearer structures on the whole and then focused work on the details, the actual writing. Those two aspects must walk hand in hand. One without the other is no good. Whether I do that here or somewhere else I don't know."

"Don't you ever get a writer's block or something? Sometimes you almost seem like a machine to me."

"It's tapping into a source, basically. There are different ways of doing this. I get a lot of ideas while daydreaming. I guess it has to do with compensatory emotions being allowed to move freely inside the realms of fantasy. And fantasy is, of course, the breeding ground of human creation. Intuition plays a major part in creative development of any kind. Courage and experimentation too. There must be plenty of room for chance and random accidents. When you're on the path, so to speak, you just have to keep walking. You have to have faith in your own juggling of supposed oppositions. In the end, nothing matters. But until then, some things do."

"OK", Mary said. "I'm happy for you. But I'd hate to see you go. Is that what you're saying? That you're here to go? Or that you're here to do? Couldn't we stay a bit longer? I mean, we've hardly met."

"You know what? If we wanted to, we could stay here forever, like you said. You may have noticed Rama has a soft spot for you. Who knows, mom, maybe he's my father? You can stay. I think you should. Do some Yoga, enjoy the mountains, enjoy Rama. I need to be on my way though. Not now of course or even soon, but at some point. Freedom must be celebrated. Money is another issue. Money must be forthcoming so that I can celebrate my freedom. Not necessarily by extravagant expressions, but by a daily appreciation of time and creativity. Work generates work, money generates money. There really shouldn't be time enough to even ruminate over the equation. As much as I love it here, it's not what I'm after right now though. I need to go a bit faster."

"What's the hurry?", Mary asked him. "Why can't you do what you need to do right here?"

"Writing, just writing. Making money, just making money. 'There is no shame, there is no guilt. This is the law: Do what thou wilt.' That was Crowley. Genius. I have so much to tap, mom. Just tap, tap tap-dance and write away. What is it I want in life? What is it I need? An increase of synchronistic happenings and meetings that will enrich my life on all levels. Networking, branching out, endorsing an open mind and an open life. Intelligence and culture entwined. Travel within and without. Making the most of opportunities, yet not selling myself cheaply."

"It seems to me you have it all together", Mary said, sighing.

Although wanting to be helpful in any way she could, she realized now that Victor was very much also a narcissistic egotist.

He just went on and on, seemingly not caring whether anyone was really listening or not. Maybe, she thought, that's something he'd developed to basically cope with being alone.

"I feel that you think I'm ranting", he said.

"Not really. I'm just a little bit tired."

"I want to read you something. I found it the other day. It's a poem I wrote in my teens. They were, as you can imagine, preoccupied with thinking about origins, identity, the core, the soul, the sun, the moon and so forth. You know what I mean, right?"

"Read it and we'll see...", Mary replied and closed her eyes.

"Self-pity, broken self-esteem
What happened to my childhood dreams?
I feel like I've been here before
We have all been here before

Frozen spirits moving up, around
Frozen lives so safe and sound
We never said it would be easy
We never aimed to try and please you

I hate the iron in you
I hate the irony in me
Forgotten by posterity
Unreachable eternity

Can we share the love that's there?
Can we share the love that's here?
Who am I to tell you what to say?
Who am I to tell me I should stay?

Don't lose faith in what we've got
What we have is still a lot
Never lose or run away
Never fail or go astray"

"It's nice. But what does it mean?", Mary began.

"Mean? It doesn't mean anything. It's just saying that I'm not running away from something but rather towards something else."

"Well, don't worry about it", Mary continued. "The main thing is that you should do what you want to and not listen too much to other people's good advice."

"Including yours, I assume?"

"Including mine. Look at you, now you have a cult of your own. Don't say all your work hasn't paid off!"

"Oh, here comes Govinda...", Rama said and got up.

A tall elderly man approached them, smiling a big smile. Apparently he'd been up trekking in the mountains, as he was carrying a backpack, a walking staff and a camera around his neck.

"Long time, Victor...", Govinda said and gave him a big hug. "Very nice to see you here again. Very, very, very nice."

"Likewise, Govinda. You've met my mother, I presume?"

"A long time ago I did have that pleasure. Very nice to see you here again too, Mary."

He turned to Rama while shaking Mary's hand.

"What a magical reunion! This is surely something to celebrate."

"Indeed", Rama said. "Have a seat and I'll get you a cup of tea. This is the beginning of the future, right here, don't you think?"

38

Over the following days, Mary and Victor took walks together, either alone or together with people from the commune. A twenty-three year old woman from Iceland, Lucy, usually joined them and it became apparent to Mary that something was brewing in the love pot. She was happy about it. If anything, Victor needed to be grounded, brought back to earth in a way. That was the mother thinking, she realized, not an acolyte filled to the brim with adoration – which was something she could see in Lucy. As a mother, she could clearly see his faults and shortcomings and was very happy to be allowed to comment on them to Victor. In fact, he seemed to appreciate her occasional criticism.

There were many small roads going higher up from the village. Some were suitable for traffic, whereas other were trekking paths. They preferred the smaller ones, and walked for hours and hours, usually up to a little cabin high up, where some Yogis took students for short-term retreats. The sun seemingly always shone, the forests were lush and dense. The air was so filled with oxygen that Mary felt her entire physical, metabolic system had changed – for the better – since she arrived.

One day they arrived at the cottage, and sat down for a pick nick. The usual problems with leeches had to be dealt with first. They ate through even the thickest boot soles and had to be removed with salt water. At first, it had revolted Mary. The creatures in themselves sucking on her flesh, and often letting her own blood when she removed them. But it was just something she got used to. Victor had no such problems, as they seemed to leave him alone. Mary asked him to teach her the trick.

"It's no trick", he said. "It's just that I have awfully smelly feet."

Looking out at the valley beneath them, they were all struck by the beauty. Beneath them, they could see the neat little village. Above them, the range just continued, seemingly endless. They really were somewhere between heaven and earth, and were often joking about exactly where that borderline was. Victor's standard answer was always, "The borderline is exactly where we are."

Some semi-wild dogs joined them as they sat down to their pick nick: Victor, Mary, Lucy, Rama and a few locals from the village. Victor liked the dogs. He patted them, although he knew they were probably flea-infested. One dog particularly caught his eye, a mixed breed female, slender and elegant despite a rugged surface. He gave the dog a severe glance. Mary could tell something was going on, and hushed the others a bit. There was some kind of telepathy going on.

"Hello, doggy. I love you and it's nice to be here with you. It's a beautiful day", Victor relayed.

"The very same to you", the dog replied in a crystal clear transmission. "Hey, did you see that UFO yesterday evening?"

Victor shook his head slowly, mystifying the human onlookers.

"A big ship hovered over the village last night. How could you miss that?"

"Probably because I was sleeping", Victor replied. "Did you catch any vibes?"

The dog nodded.

"Sure. Good vibes all around. I think they simply want to check out what you're up to. And, by the way, I don't think they're alone in that respect."

"Meaning what?", Victor asked.

"You need to open your eyes a bit more, buddy. There have been some white strangers in the area lately. Not interested in trekking, if you catch my drift."

"I see", Victor replied. "Do you think it's the village or that UFO that they're after?"

"Both and neither", the dog answered and drank some water that Victor had poured her on a plate. "I think they're also curious to check you out, and you are, or possibly could be, the link stuck in between."

Victor noticed how the others were dead silent and looking at him and the dog.

"Hey! I'm still here!", the dog snarled. "So, now you know. By the way, that woman is not a bad looker..."

"You mean Lucy? Yes, she's nice."

"Nice? You idiot. Impregnate her now before someone else does or before the UFO gets her. I know for a fact they're collecting human females in the region."

"Really? And your advice is that I screw her?"

"You mean you haven't already? You may have your cosmic mojo working, Mr. Human All Too Human Wizard, but now is the time to get that real mojo working too. What are you waiting for?"

Victor took a sip of coffee from his cup. The dog went away, followed by the others.

"Wow, Victor, what was that all about?", Mary asked.

"That dog is a bit more than just a friend", he replied.

"We could see that", Lucy said. "Just don't say that you're lovers! What did it want?"

Victor looked at her, got up and took her by the hand. They went inside the cottage, which was a little bit away.

"Lucy", he began. "Lucy, I don't know where to begin without sounding really, really strange. You see, sometimes in life..."

She signaled to him to be silent and started rubbing his penis quite aggressively. As they interlocked in a tantric position called "Padmasambava's pineal knot" on the simple bed (having brushed off spiders and other insects first), they could hear the dogs barking and howling in the distance. As Victor ejaculated inside Lucy and his spasms almost made the bed collapse, his inner eye could indeed see a huge spaceship hovering over the region, completely invisible yet glowing with unearthly colors. The dog was right all along, Victor thought, as he exhaled in that lovingly volcanic Icelandic embrace.

39

Every day at noon, Victor received visitors who were curious. Most of these were just tourists passing through, settling in for a few days to attend Yoga classes and enjoy the scenery. His presence wasn't advertised in any way, but apparently the word was out in Kathmandu.

Mary sometimes sat close by, to watch and listen to what was going on. Sometimes it was just one or two people and sometimes groups of ten. Sometimes journalists showed up too, usually Westerners who were based in Bangkok and looking for a story they could sell. Victor was always courteous and seemed to project back more or less exactly what they were after. How he could know what they were after seemed a mystery to Mary, but she realized that perhaps he was just a good "reader" of people's expectations and personalities. She had seen examples of this before on TV, with actors who were used to giving a million interviews, yet always able to make each interviewer feel right at home and special.

They talked about it at times. Mary wondered why he didn't get tired of the attention.

"Sometimes I do", Victor confessed. "But you've surely noticed that I enjoy it too. Perhaps I even need it. Attention-craving is a common trait in kids with distant parents, you know. And my parents were indeed distant or, rather, non-existent."

Mary felt bad when he said things like that. Although they'd already gone over it many times by now and although she could recognize his ironic tone, it was still painful to hear.

"But aren't you just feeding them what they want to hear?", she asked. "Do you really feel that you're always telling them something that's of use to them?"

"Ah, can I detect a slight criticism there, mom? To tell you the truth, who am I to tell the truth? They ask, I reply. How could I do more than that? One thing I've learned though: to speak clearly is quite often not the best way. As you've noticed, some people find me cryptic and self-indulgent. You know what? They're absolutely right. If I were to adapt the expressions of what I feel and think to each person's expectations, then I'd be even more self-indulgent. I just do what I do and say what I say."

"I see", Mary said. "Look, I know you're really wise and all, and I don't mean to criticize you. You've given a lot of things a lot of thought. I'm proud of you."

"Thanks. Again, it's impossible to be who you're not. You can try, like you tried, but I guess everyone comes to a critical point when it becomes impossible, unbearable. I've been fortunate, in that I've been able to develop my mind freely, under the guidance of beautiful and spiritually inclined people like Big Baba and Rama and many of the other magicians I met later on. But perhaps it was you who actually paid the price for that. Your not coming back perhaps enabled me to grow in this direction. If that's the case – and we'll never really know, will we? – then I'm very grateful. And, by the way, I'm sure you're wise and that you've given a lot of things a lot of thought too."

"Sure", Mary said. "Of that you can be sure. And the original decision, or whatever we should call it, was mine after all. I mean, to not come back."

"I know", Victor continued. "That's why I haven't even bothered with thinking too much about the father issue. If your story is true, wouldn't it be great to know which of the Fateful Heads I stem from? But that doesn't really change anything. Here we are and of that we can be pretty sure, or at least as sure as two human beings can be, sharing a more or less common perspective. Maybe that's quite enough, at least to begin with?"

There was silence. Mary felt the same way and the sun was setting, painting everything around them in an ethereal golden glow.

40

"I think we should have a party", Victor said. "I'm getting a little tired of all the daily routines. Think about it. It could bring some attention to what we're doing here."

Rama seemed pensive. He was accustomed to the daily quiet grind of the serene village and its routines.

"You mean with drinking and dancing?", he asked. "I'm not so sure that would be a good idea."

"Why not? Let the people do what they want to do. I think it's a great idea. Rama, I really don't know how long I want to stay here this time. I love it, I do, and don't worry, I'll come back. But I feel we should celebrate somehow. It'll be Party Yoga. Also, I'm sure a lot of people from Kathmandu would come to. You know, old friends, new friends. Think about it."

"Yes, let me think about it.", Rama answered. "I'm not totally against it but I can't say I'm totally for it either."

"That's the spirit, Rama", Victor said and laughed.

41

It didn't take much persuasion to get everyone enthusiastic, including Rama. Soon preparations were under way. Govinda Harrer came back often from his treks, lit up at the idea and suggested the necessary practical and technical solutions, while Victor cheered everyone on. It would be a low-key event, he said, and it should be allowed to develop in what he called "intuitive directions". No one really understood what he meant, but they all looked forward to it. Mary thought it was great too, and Rama realized that maybe it wasn't such a bad idea after all. Secretly, he feared growing older and getting stuck in so called "normality". This could perhaps become a boost of youthful energy?

"Rama", Victor said as he entered the office of their village compound. "Do we know anyone with connections in the psychedelic world? I mean, in Kathmandu."

"Are you thinking about the party?", Rama asked.

"That's right. We should at least let people choose what they want to do. I don't mind drinking but we should also have a little something to spice things up a bit, don't you think?"

"I'll see what I can do", Rama said. "I have a nephew in town who might be able to help out."

"Wonderful. Don't worry, Rama, we'll have a party that will be remembered for a long time. I know Govinda is preparing something extra special too."

42

There was a bus coming up to the village every morning. Locals who lived further down the hill, tourists and new students arrived to catch the villagers waking up and planning for the day.

This specific morning brought someone Victor could spot from miles away. As he had his morning coffee together with Lucy and Mary on the main building's patio, he stood up to see if it was really her. As the dust from the leaving bus settled in, he could see Ilse Grokmann standing there, looking straight at him.

"Well, well, fancy meeting you here...", he began.

"This is the Patanjali place, isn't it?"

"It certainly is. PSYNC, the Patanjali Society for Yoga and Neophile Culture. I'm surprised you could find me. Honored, even. How was Bangkok?"

"Not my cup of tea. I told you, I'm more interested in the human mind."

"There are plenty of human minds in Bangkok", Victor continued.

"Sure. But I'm more interested in your mind. You know that, don't you? Couldn't we please start over? I would so very much like to talk to you."

Victor offered her a seat and brought her breakfast. Mary and Lucy welcomed her too.

"Thanks. I'm really genuinely interested in the human mind. You believe me, don't you?", Grokmann asked Victor.

"You don't have to explain anything. We're all interested in the human mind here, aren't we? The difference, I guess, is in which approach we choose. Eat and relax, Ilse, and I'll show you around afterwards."

43

After having walked and talked with her, Victor suggested that Grokmann should stay a while, do some yoga and talk to the teachers while experimenting on herself. If she was truly interested, there was only one way to learn. That was to do and not only to read or ask. Although hesitant at first, Grokmann agreed.

Victor told her everything would be fine. Provided she stuck to the rules of the PSYNC, that is. He had a hunch she wouldn't, but was more than willing to give her a chance to prove him wrong.

44

Some evenings later on, Rama closed the door to his office and Victor sat down by the desk. Rama's nephew, Indra, who had just arrived from Kathmandu, smiled at them and opened his bag. He brought out a big plastic package filled with marijuana.

"Oh, that will be more then enough, I think", Victor said. "And the booze?"

"Yes, I fixed that too", Indra said. "No problem. There will be a truck with beer and wine and spirits. No problem."

"How are we going to deal with this?", Rama sighed.

"Don't worry. It's a feast for the Gods and they demand intoxication. You know that."

"Then there was this...", Indra said.

He brought out three small vials containing a clear liquid. Victor and Rama each took one to look at.

"You have got to be kidding!", Victor whispered. "Sandoz Laboratories, LSD-25... From last year! How the hell did you get this?"

"Many friends", Indra smiled. "Many friends. So you want?"

"Want? Indra, you just changed this from a party to a ritual celebration in Shiva's honor. How much does it cost?"

"The grass is very cheap. The alcohol is very expensive. Those bottles are free."

Victor and Indra hugged. Victor looked at Rama who was still looking at the small vial, smiling.

“How should we deal with this?”, Rama asked again as they were stashing everything away.

“We’ll make some kind of fruit punch and tell people to have a drink if they want to”, Victor replied.

“You mean telling them or not? Spiking drinks used to be a very immoral thing, Victor.”

“I know that and of course it still is. We’ll just have to hint. We’ll call the punch ‘Amrita’ or ‘Shiva’s Lightning’ or ‘Yin-Yang Special’ or ‘Third Eye Potion’ or something like that. Just like in the old days, eh? Sometimes free will and moral dilemmas need a little push in the right direction. We’re doing this for a good cause too, remember, so the Gods won’t judge us too harshly.”

45

“Have a seat, Ilse. How are things? Are you finding anything that’s interesting?”, Victor asked her.

“Yes. It’s hard work, though. I’m used to other methods, that’s all.”

“I can tell you one thing that clinical psychology or empirical science can’t. There’s one ingredient that needs to be there: a sincerity that’s not based in greed. Know what I mean? The main reason why so much proto-science has been kept from scientists is simply that they haven’t been mature enough to receive the specific knowledge.”

“What are you talking about? Kept from scientists by whom? One only finds out by doing something over and over again until it works. That’s science.”

“No, what you’re talking about is an accumulation of statistics. That’s not the same thing, Ilse. I could give you all the information you want, and I would if I could only sense that you’d put it to some other use than warfare or control or petty greed.”

“I’d never do that! I’m a scientist!”, Grokmann said.

“I know. I don’t doubt the sincerity of your self-image or your will. What I do doubt is your own individual vision or your emotional sincerity. Would you like to hear a secret?”

“Can I record this?”, Grokmann asked.

“I certainly hope you’re joking. That’s exactly what I mean.

Just sit back and relax. I will tell you some secrets. You can do with them what you please. OK?"

Grokmann looked at Victor enthusiastically and nodded.

"Honesty is a key to this, Ilse. To everything. You can't be creative in any field whatsoever – and I include science in that – if you're not honest to yourself. A long time ago, I formulated myself, basically for myself only. Like a declaration of my will, a formulation, a decree, an existential to-do list... Although it's mine and mine alone, I don't mind sharing this now. You can make of it whatever you want.

I want the courage and audacity to believe in my creative forces as sustainers as well as artistic expressions. A genuine and wholehearted attitude towards everything and everyone around me. It's from the inside out, not vice versa.

Synchronicities galore – the essence of magic.

Massage and physical activities in moderation but still more than they are present today.

Capturing faces and human destinies for posterity. Emotional documentation. I never expected access could be so easy. A mutual trust that I would never misuse.

Causal wealth: One thing leads to another, always.

An immediate, intuitive sense of photographic composition. A snapshot can become a monument if I so desire.

Financial control. If wealth, prosperity and affluence bring a greater sense of non-distraction and a possibility to focus more on the artistic process, then there's nothing wrong with them.

'Kunst und Geist'. A spiritual contemplative presence.

Being loved and being aware of it. Loving and being aware of it. Being aware in general and loving it.

Response and success on all creative fronts. Intelligent feedback and selective dialogues.

Help where and when it's needed. If I'm weak in selling whatever it is I'm doing, I need agents, galleries etc to help. Magically, they manifest, believe in me and work for developing long-term commitments. An ideal situation where I am happily left to create the essential.

Detachment and joy according to my inspirational elders. Mirth and chuckle.

Wasting nothing, no time and no one. However, waste management is not the ultimate key: focused proto-work is..."

Grokmann looked up at him. Victor couldn't be sure she understood what this was. He wasn't entirely sure he understood everything himself.

"Thanks", she said. "I think I get it. You gave me yourself there. Or a piece of yourself."

"That's it. And the key is not in who I am or what I said or what I claimed that I want in life. The key is that I mean every word, every letter, and that I was willing to share that with you. Now do you understand me? Can you apply that attitude to your science? If so, you'll be fine, Ilse. If not, then I probably can't help you."

"I think I understand", Grokmann replied. "It's about being open for suggestion? Open for being open?"

"That sounds just right", Victor replied. "But enough of that now, Ilse. Now, or at least very soon, is party time. Relax and enjoy life. You've deserved that."

46

"OK, so you know what to do now?", Special Agent Buck Rover of the US Embassy in Kathmandu asked Junior Special Agent Janus Hogger, incidentally also a student of Yoga at the PSYNC village.

"As you can move about freely there, we're counting on you. You find their drinks and then assess the best way. Either it's in plastic bottles and then you'll have to use these syringes and inject. That's complicated, I know, but you can at least try. Or it'll be in bowls or containers of some kind. If they have punch in bowls, it's easy: you just pour one small vial in each bowl. You don't have to be super-diligent about it. The main thing is that at least a couple of bottles or bowls or whatever contain this liquid. Is that understood?"

"Sure", the young agent replied. "What is it? It's not going to kill them or anything?"

"No, of course not! What do you think we are, some kind of fucking barbarians? No, it's LSD."

"LSD? Acid? Wow! Groovy...", the young man exclaimed.

"Groovy?", Rover said. "I sincerely hope you are joking."

"Uh, yes. Sorry. I just mean that spiking used to be an immoral thing in those circuits."

"Immoral? Look, we have a job to do and sometimes it isn't pretty. Live with that, play by the book and some kind of promotion will be there for you. Get it? I know spiking is immoral but if we don't do this then who will? Sometimes free will and moral dilemmas need a little push in the right direction. We're doing this for a good cause too, remember. No committee or commission will ever know. Am I making myself clear?"

"Yes Sir, as clear as the liquid in those bottles, Sir!", the young agent replied and stood in firm attention, already making plans to secure some of that LSD for himself.

47

"Dearly beloved of all faiths and creeds. I'm happy to be here again, after such a long trip…"

Victor began a little hesitantly, eyeing the large crowd who seemed nothing but happy to be there. A party this size was not at all usual up in the hills, so an assortment of people had shown up: old-timers, gurus, babas, young backpackers, students at the village, local Nepalese and many others. Victor's silence increased their anticipation and he noticed it.

"I never thought I'd say it, but now I do. Listen to my voice. Am I talking to you or not? Are my words inside your head now? If they are, can you make them disappear? I think not. It's not a problem, is it? You don't mind me being there, do you? Just relax for a while. Take a deep breath. When you wake up you will eventually fall asleep again and then you will remember everything. Almost everything. Listen to my voice.

I remember all those magical nights spent in union with everyone and everything. We were setting new standards for art and for the future, turning into magicians without knowing it. The stars were our thoughts and ideas and all our heartbeats shared one cosmic rhythm. It has never stopped. It is still there. It is still here. We have work to do. Let's never forget that. The show must go on with the show.

Although we're here in a tradition that's Hindu in essence, perhaps Buddhist too, I think we should pay our respects to everyone from everywhere who's fought for freedom in life and in mind. I'd like to read a little poem I wrote a long time ago, to open the festivities, and then we should have a really good time. What do you say?"

Everyone present cheered loudly and applauded, including Mary.

"Alright. It's called 'Lucifer's Rainbow' and it goes something like this…

People of the towns
People of the forests
Come on down together
Tonight we have been blessed

Step into the circle
Step inside your mind
Step into the mazes
And step outside of time

Why they won't allow us
Is as clear as starry skies
Hidden in the darkness
We dance away their lies

Our hands are joined together
Sworn to nature's powers
Sworn to care forever
For all the little flowers

Well inside our circle
We open up and feel
A love that grows between us
A love becoming real

As destiny grabs us
And shows us who we are
We cry out in the night

And hope to go on far

Lucifer's Rainbow
Shine a light on me
All the things that I know
Here to set you free

Lucifer's Rainbow
Shine a light on me
All the things that you know
Here to set me free"

The crowd roared and applauded when it was over. Mary noticed how Victor discretely nodded to Rama, who in turn nodded to some others. Within seconds, fireworks lit up the darkening Himalayan sky and everyone knew the party had really started.

Victor came down from the small stage and gave Mary and then Rama a big hug. Others wanted to be in on it too, so it became a nice moment of mutual love for all involved.

The night was dark yet still warm. People drifted around the area, dancing, talking, looking at the starry sky. The DJ, the famous Osho Gosh, played psychedelic rock from the 1960s and the usually long-winding guitar solos echoed diligently over the entire Himalayan landscape.

Govinda Harrer hurried around and gave orders to his technical team. Everyone looked forward to his magic. He was something of a wizard on the outdoor party scene all over Asia, always creating new wonders. He had promised that this night would be very special.

Victor drifted around slowly, greeting people with a beatific smile. He looked high, but Mary knew he really wasn't. Or was he? He was just coming into his own, at this very moment. Occasional glances between her and Rama confirmed to each other that they were witnessing something important.

Lucy joined in and took Victor by the hand. They smiled at each other. Mary was overwhelmed by a feeling of happiness, as if the surroundings and the reunion wasn't enough. Lucy whispered something in Victor's ear and he nodded at her.

He made a gesture to Osho Gosh and climbed up on the stage

again. More cheering from the crowd. He tapped on the microphone to ensure he was heard.

"Hey, Osho, could you put some delay on my voice? I want this to be heard properly. Thanks..."

His voice suddenly echoed and people laughed and screamed with childlike satisfaction at the psychedelic indulgence.

"Dearly beloved, we are gathered here tonight...", he started slowly. "Before we proceed with Govinda Harrer's illuminated blessings, I have been asked to read another poem. But which poem? To read something old would perhaps be boring? To read something new would perhaps be appropriate. But I'm going to delve even further than that. This poem is from the future – perhaps – and it's dedicated to each and everyone present here tonight, and to Lucy, who is also present here tonight. It's called 'The future':

Gliding down that silent, dirty river
Grass and trees and hot and humid air
No one sees me here but naked strangers
Now I wish that you were really, really here
Sliding down that well-known lonely shiver
Feet and hands and all their dirty hair
No one sees me here but naked strangers
How I wish that I was really, really there

Taking in the color-forms of flowers
They greet me as the sun goes down to rest
There's no one here to show me that I'm living
Only voices from the past are being blessed

I know my sinking ship is safe and sound now
I go ashore and move myself right up ahead
A new life in the good old magic kingdom
I close my eyes and slowly go right back to bed

Hey, mister, carry your own backpack or I'll shut my eyes
Hey, sister, sort out your own mess or I'll shut my ears
This is my jungle, my desert, my flowers, my dirt
For those who cannot see that, I'll shut my...

I'll shut my... I'll shut my... My Magic Kingdom

I wake up and I walk on through the jungle
To the desert where my ship will soon set sail
Waves of many bitter tears release me
And I dream that this time I refuse to fail

So I glide on down that golden bloody river
Forgetting what it was that I once sought
And I'm back again from seconds of exploring
The world was so much smaller than we thought"

He paused. People were awestruck. What did it all mean? Then Lucy started jumping and applauding like a madwoman and everyone followed her example. Someone yelled "More!", and Victor looked up at the sky.

"You're insatiable", he said. "Maybe that's good? We have yet to see. I don't have any poems from the future left, so you'll have to make do with one from the very now... This one is called 'The Sun of Man':

The sun is warm, we're loving who we are
My body's like a heaven and my mind is like a star
I spin around forever and hope to land some day
The sun of man will feed me in a very special way

We build a house with a roof of solid hope
Live and love together, it seems that we can cope
I never said we could make these our own dreams
But we did, or so it seems

The sun of man exploded yesterday
No time to see and no time to play
We flew on over and tried to move on by
A bigger picture turned out to be a lie

All our friends came over to shake our dirty hands
No place for flowers and no place for lands
As we were leaving they told us what to do

Sow the seeds of love and cherish what is true

All our fallen heroes are coming back to life
Hungrier than ever and looking for a wife
Who could have known that silence was a key
The silence I am singing for those who care to see

You said you knew me and maybe that's all right
The sun of man exploded in a fight
We walk on through the grass, happy as can be
Enjoying to the fullest what it feels like to be free

The sun of man exploded yesterday
No time to see and no time to play
We flew on over and tried to move on by
A bigger picture turned out to be a lie

All our friends came over to shake our dirty hands
No place for flowers and no place for lands
As we were leaving they told us what to do
Sow the seeds of love and cherish what is true"

More applause. The crowd was going absolutely wild. Mary was crying and Rama handed her some tissue paper.

"OK, everybody... Osho, Govinda, are we ready?"

"Yes, we're ready!", Govinda Harrer shouted loudly in his German accent as Victor descended from the stage.

Close by the stage was an area filled with weird machines and projectors. Govinda Harrer was now placed in the center by his computer, very much looking like the mad scientist. He signaled to Osho Gosh and all his assistants to get ready.

Suddenly some electronic ambient music was heard over the sound system. People looked up at the stars, holding hands and waiting to be mind-blown yet again. A strange hiss was heard and people could see that incredibly fine humidity was sprayed over yet another area, like an entire wall or screen of delicate water. Slowly, colors began pulsating on the surface of this wall – psychedelic patterns, grids, fractals, complementary colors swirling in an overwhelming cosmic dance.

Some of Harrer's assistants were out in the crowd with small video cameras. As out of nowhere, these images were softly mixed in and people could suddenly see their own faces superimposed and projected on this evanescent texture of pure water. One of the cameras zoomed in on Victor and Lucy, who watched their own faces becoming larger than life.

"Lucy in the sky!", Victor shouted and everyone laughed and screamed.

The soundtrack gradually became more rhythmic. The images were now 1960s and 70s footage from Nepal, religious icons, shrines, Buddhist tangkas, hippies shot on Super-8, wildlife and occasional super impositions of people present watching, their eyes and minds almost unbelieving of this miasmic eye-candy bonanza.

Victor got closer to Mary. They embraced but didn't let go of the cosmic screen with their eyes. Early footage of The Fateful Head was presented in slow motion and suddenly it was very apparent that some of it was shot in Kathmandu, also on Super-8. The band's music could now be heard through the sound system. There they all were: the band, Mosely-Manly, a bunch of happy hippies and hilarious hang-arounds, gathered to celebrate life and the psychedelic experience on the rooftops of Thamel. Mary started crying when she, and everyone else, saw slow-moving images of herself and Sparkles: beautiful young American girls in the midst of a rock'n'roll entourage destined to change her life forever. She smiled at the camera. The strong colors and the dust on the film evoked everything at once. She looked at Victor. He too was crying.

"One of those men is your father", Mary whispered into his ear.

"No. I know you think so, but it's actually all of them," he replied, leaving her slightly puzzled.

The soundtrack drifted back to electronic sounds and Victor recognized it immediately: it was Blaxpots' highly appraised piece "Oysters are for suckers". The images changed. The sun rising over the Himalayas was super imposed with his currently crying face. Not a dry eye in the crowd. The Nepalese and Tibetan flags superimposed over the steady mountain range. Mount Kailash (that Victor had at one point visited) immersed in the rays of the morning sun. Lake Manasarovar, close to Kailash, super imposed with images of Nordic runes, Hebrew letters, Sanskrit, and magical signs from esoteric history. He had shot the footage of Kailash and Manasarovar himself, he remembered, and left it with Harrer some twenty years ago. Then a close-up of the Dalai Lama's smiling face merging with that of the Swiss chemist Albert Hofmann, which then dissolved into a million multicolored fragments. The projection then changed back to Harrer's special treat of cosmic patterns, and eventually ended with a slow fading out. The crowd could see the actual waterwall again, and then nothing.

The silence was overwhelming. People couldn't move or say a word. Osho was looking at Victor, who signaled silence. He walked over to Govinda Harrer and gave him a long hug. And the people started screaming again. And Osho Gosh started spinning acid rock again, even louder this time around.

Mary joined them, as did Lucy and Rama. Victor still held Govinda in embrace. When he eventually let go, he looked Mary in the eyes.

"Didn't I just say that nothing remains until it's time to start over?", Victor started, cryptically. "I wish that someone would listen, just for once. Did you listen? Not that I care but I do think that you should. Of all the things we said and did, does anything in particular stand out? I'm not so certain anymore. Gone today, here tomorrow, and all the romantic notions of a glorious past filled with exactly the same things, over and over. In the end, nothing matters. But until then, some things do."

"Are you high, baby?", Mary asked him, slightly worried.

"You bet I am", he replied and smiled. "We may have been spiked, but I don't know by whom. By us? By them? We are grateful, no matter what. Don't call me baby, by the way."

48

Deep in the night people continued dancing and having a good old Dionysian time. As before, Victor drifted in and out of smaller groups, talking, hugging, shaking hands. Mary could see him at a distance, vaguely resembling a politician of some political system that hadn't been invented yet: a direct transfer of ideas into the minds and hearts of people.

Rama asked if she wanted something to drink. They sat down some distance away from the loud music. Rama handed her a glass of lemonade and they sat down to watch the spectacle.

"He seems to be at home...", Rama began. "How are you? How do you feel?"

Mary sat silent for a while, thinking about the question. Just one week earlier, she had been at home in the US, hesitant, not knowing what to believe or believe in. Now all of a sudden she was in the Himalayas again, reunited with her long lost son and in the middle of a cosmic feast that brought back memories from her youth.

"To tell you the truth, Rama, I don't know. It's a little bit much to take in."

"Don't worry," Rama said and laid his arm around her. "Who knows anything anyway? I care about your happiness though. You can stay here and be happy as long as you want."

"I know. I've heard that before, remember? That in itself makes me happy. I just can't understand that any of this is actually true, that it is actually happening. Have I been dreaming all along?"

Rama laughed. They shared the drink and it felt good, cooling, refreshing. The crowd seemed far away and the sounds were muffled, as if coming from a great distance. People were dancing as one mass of unified life force, creating an ethereal glow that lit up the entire village.

"Maybe we're all dreaming this," Rama continued. "We were here then, you know, and we're here now. So is Victor, so is Lucy, so is Govinda Harrer and everyone else. Beautiful people. Beautiful friends. If we're here now, it must all be true, right? But a dream is no less true than what we see with our eyes, right? Think about it. I remember a poem that Victor wrote when he was seven. He brought it to my father, who read it aloud to everyone at that time. I still remember it:

The way it once was, all over again
We can never change what happened way back when
Take a look at what you've done

The way it once was, now that it's gone"

"What? He wrote that when he was seven?", Mary asked.

"Yes, very good poem, right?"

"Sure. It's absolutely beautiful. Maybe a little sad too."

"Not an ordinary child. Not an ordinary mother."

Rama suddenly gave Mary a hug and then they kissed for what seemed to Mary like an eternity. A very pleasant eternity, she realized. Then they looked at each other for a long time without speaking.

"Rama...", Mary said softly after a while. "I don't quite know how to say this. Your face is alive. Actually, very alive."

"So is yours," Rama whispered.

"Are you doing some magic to me?", she asked.

"Not really, it's probably just the acid."

"But I haven't taken any. It's been almost 40 years."

"Oh, there was some in this lemonade I think. I'm sure of it. 40 years is nothing, Mary. The planet has existed for many billions of years. But now you're back. Back in Nepal, back on the planet..."

Mary watched the crowd again. A multicolored vortex was rising from the crowd's center, like those DNA helixes she had seen on TV. The vortex shifted shape like some kind of benevolent tornado of love, spreading out, re-uniting, with changing bright colors like Christmas lights.

"You know what, Rama... I think I actually just left the planet..."

They burst out laughing hysterically and then wandered slowly back to the center of the mass, giggling like small children on a mischievous adventure.

Time passed, as it usually does. The party went on. The stars were so bright that most of the people looked up rather than at the psychedelic lightshow of Govinda Harrer. Even he himself looked up. If ever there was a night of beauty and ecstasy, this was it, he thought to himself and remembered his own childhood in the Swiss Alps. Some people had retired, some were busy making love, but most of them were still dancing and frolicking. Even the local Nepalese had joined in and danced in their own traditional way.

49

Out of the dark suddenly emerged some khaki-clad Nepalese soldiers, led by Western men, and several cars drove up and blocked the road. Panic ensued, not so much in screaming but in nervous movements. As this was a peaceful crowd, they just decided to stay put. Osho Gosh killed the sound and Harrer blasted all lights so that everyone could see everything and each other.

"No need for alarm!", someone shouted in an American accent. "No one's going to get hurt. Who's in charge here?"

A Nepalese officer translated but the locals kept quiet.

"No one's in charge!", Victor shouted. "Are you in charge?"

People started laughing. Before any kind of violent reaction could ensue, Victor quickly approached the American, who looked more like an desk clerk than a military man. Rama was right by his side.

"We have reason to believe there are drugs here", the official said. "We intend to search the area and make arrests."

"You have already arrested our party", Victor said. "Since when is it a crime to have some fun?"

"I would strongly advise you to shut up, Mr. Ritterstadt."

"You know my name? Now, isn't that a coincidence?"

"Oh yeah, why is that?", the official said aggressively. "Never mind. Gather up all the drinks, all the bowls, bottles and glasses!"

The Nepalese soldiers ran around the area and brought back everything to a van. People just watched in amazement, afraid of possible violence but also giggling at the same time at the insane comedy of it all.

"We have reason to believe there are drugs involved here", the official repeated. "The party is over, Ritterstadt."

"If I were you, Rover, I wouldn't be so sure", Victor replied.

"How the hell do you know my name?"

"It says on that badge", Victor said and pointed to the identity card Rover carried around his neck.

"Oh. Anyway, the party's over. Everyone go home right now!"

"But they already are home", Victor continued.

People were beginning to laugh quietly again, and this, of course, didn't improve the diplomatic relations.

Rover and his entourage of overt secret agents and Nepalese

soldiers secured the area by posting soldiers here and there. Most people were silent, watching the eerie spectacle with disdain. From inside a house, laughter and voices could be heard. Rover entered the house together with one of the Nepalese soldiers.

The sounds came from a small room at the back.

"Be careful, very careful", Rover whispered to the soldier.

As they entered the small room, they could see Junior Agent Hogger in bed with a Western woman, both stark naked. They both burst out laughing even more when they saw Rover and his concerned face.

"Rover, goddamnit, good to see you, Sir... As you can see, I'm under cover...", Hogger said and pulled a blanket over their naked bodies, laughing hysterically.

"I want you to come with me right this minute!", Rover shouted aggressively.

Hogger pulled the blanket down again and looked at his superior officer.

"I'm sorry Sir, but I'm not gay", the young man roared. "And besides, I just came... It's too late!"

The walls were shaking with the young couple's laughter. Rover sighed and left. The Nepalese soldier looked at him and then followed. These Western people are all crazy, he thought.

50

Suddenly they could all hear dogs frantically howling and barking nearby. It startled everybody, and the Nepalese soldiers used flashlights so they could find and perhaps shoot a few wild dogs. But very soon, they had other things on their minds.

The ground started to tremble and people immediately clutched each other's arms in fear and desperation. There was a low monotonous sound and everyone looked at Osho Gosh, who screamed it wasn't him. And then a soft red light lit up the entire area. They looked up. The sky was red, glowing orange-red like fire, pulsating in flashes that could be seen, heard and felt. There was heat, strong heat. No one moved. People were completely stuck: the students, the locals, the Nepalese soldiers, the agents, the American official and Victor Ritterstadt. They all just looked up at the throbbing red sky, not knowing what to do. Everyone seemed to be sweating and praying they wouldn't die. Victor slowly went over to Mary and Lucy to comfort them. They said they were feeling dizzy.

"Don't be afraid", Victor whispered. "It's just a UFO."

Everyone was completely awestruck by the experience, including Ilse Grokmann. They would never believe this in Berlin! She suddenly felt a hand on her shoulder. It was Victor. He whispered something in her ear and she looked at him and nodded. He smiled at her and urged her on. Then she walked straight out towards the center of the red light. No one said anything. There was an increase of light and energy in the center and suddenly Ilse Grokmann was gone. Disappeared, just like that.

Then slowly the light grew dimmer. The sound receded. As if nothing had happened, the dark night sky was filled with stars again and the crickets could be heard, with occasional affirmative dog barks. Rover looked around in panic and tried using his mobile phone, in vain. People hugged each other and started smiling again. No one really knew what to say.

"You have a phone here?", Rover asked and Rama went with him to the office building.

"It's OK", Victor shouted. "It's OK. Everyone's friends now."

He went over to the Nepalese soldiers, who looked nervous and afraid. He greeted them. Most of them were very young and trembling with fear. This had been something else than the crowd control they were used to.

"Hey Lucy, bring some glasses to our friends", Victor shouted and waved her over.

The soldiers sweated profusely. Usually, the Himalayan nights were cold but the thing in the sky had heated up everything and everyone. Lucy gave them glasses and they filled them from the bowls and drank.

Rover came out again after a while, joined by Rama. No phone had worked. Silence. But the tension was gone, even Rover could feel that. The crickets played a soothing symphony of nocturnal beauty.

"What the hell happened, Parsons?", Rover asked one of his team members.

"I have no idea. Your guess is as good as mine", the man replied in a distinct British accent. “But I know that no one will ever believe us if we talk about this. They’ll think we are out of our minds or something.”

Rover noticed that Parsons drank from a glass in heavy gulps.

“Where did that drink come from?”, Rover asked him. “You didn’t drink from that bowl, did you?”

“I most certainly did, Rover. Do you have a problem with that? Do you know something that I don’t?”

“I’m just saying we should be careful. There’s drugs in that bowl”, he whispered.

“It amazes me how you can know that before it’s even tested”, Parsons replied. “Actually, I’m testing it myself right now and I hope and pray there’s some good shit in it, whatever it may be. By the way, did you notice an hour actually passed?”

Rover looked at his watch. It said 4.30 in the morning. They had arrived at the village at 3.15, which was, in his mind, fifteen minutes ago. Then whatever it was that had happened had happened. But that was only like a flash, a couple of minutes, he thought.

“What do you say if we stay a little while?”, Parsons suggested. “I think it might be a good idea.”

Rover nodded. He was very tired and very hot. When Parsons handed him a drink of spiked punch, he downed it in a second and asked for another. What the hell, he thought. The agent he had talked to in Brussels had said it was very clean and that accidental intake was completely harmless, unless accidentally repeated. Being thirsty, Rover just didn’t give a damn anymore.

“You’re all very welcome to stay”, Rama told them. The sun will be rising soon, and after that we’ll make some nice breakfast for everyone. Just put the guns away and everything will be fine. Victor, can I have a word with you?”

Victor and Rama walked away slowly and kept talking.

“You gave the space people that woman?”, Rama asked.

“I’d say she gave herself to the space people. In the name of science, of course. She’ll be fine, I hope. We should probably worry more about the space people. They’ll have their hands or their tentacles full of Ilse.”

“Did you...?”, Rama began and looked around. “Did you see what they left?”

Victor shook his head. Rama showed him a piece of metal or alloy that was hard and greyish yet very light.

"This came from them?", Victor asked.

"Yes. Fell right down by my feet, out of the blue... Out of the red... What do you think it is?"

"I have no idea. But if it's from them, we should take it seriously. If it's something good, we'll be thankful to Ilse Grokmann. And if it's something bad, we can blame her instead. It's all relative, just like her scientific mind, I guess."

Rama hid the strange thing in his pocket and they walked back towards the crowd. Lucy and Mary had already started bringing out bread and fruit and others were making tea in large pots. The night was mellow and peaceful. Some kind of stupefied silence reigned supreme.

51

"Who shot that beautiful footage?", Mary asked Govinda when they woke up late the next day.

They had been sleeping in the same room because the village had been so crowded.

"I mean, from the party. It was incredible. I don't think I've ever seen something that beautiful."

"I'm happy you liked it. It's mine actually. I shot it. I've kept it and never shown it to anyone."

"What? You filmed that? You were at that party?"

"Yes", Govinda continued. "It was a great time. I have pictures too, photos. I'll show them to you some time. And Victor too."

"That's amazing, Govinda. You probably have photos of him growing up too, then? I would love to see them. It's strange I can't remember you from the party."

"Is it?", Govinda asked and smiled. "I think you were starstruck and busy with the band. Everyone was, I can remember that. And with Mosely-Manly too, of course. It was a very special occasion in so many ways. I knew that I had to document it. Memory fades, but photos will last a bit longer. At least I hope so."

"I can't remember you from later either", Mary said. "Were you here at the village also?"

"No", Govinda replied. "I traveled. I didn't get to see you again. When I came back, you were gone."

"But you met Victor?"

"Sure. I've always lived here off and on, and I still do, as you know. I taught Victor about photography, literature and music. He was a very good student."

"So you were the one who got him started in everything? Wow... I'm very happy about that."

"So am I. He's good too. I'm proud of him. He needs to center himself a bit still, but I can see that coming."

"And the magic?", Mary asked. "Does that interest you too? Do you believe in it?"

"Magic lies in creation", Govinda answered. "Everyone can experience the wonders of the mind. Not everyone can express what they find in ways that will touch people's hearts."

"You really are an artist, Govinda. I'm so happy that you were there for Victor. You and Big Baba and Rama, all of you."

"We're still here for him, each in different ways. Now, if you'll excuse me, I have some work to do."

52

Special Agent Rover had been tripping all through the day after the party. He stayed on with most of his men, watched the sun rise over the mountain ridge and enjoyed breakfast and the company at the village. They strolled, laughed, talked, drew pictures, tried writing a bit in notebooks but mainly enjoyed the scenery. For Rover, it was almost like being back in College again. They all remembered the spacecraft, if that was what it was. No one was really keen to talk about it though.

Later the following evening, when Rover was settled and relaxed in his Kathmandu bungalow, he felt straight enough to try and make sense of what had happened. But he couldn't. He settled for that. The next day he would make contact with Ritterstadt again though, for the sake of protocol.

The following morning, after a good, heavy sleep, Rover

called Rama and let him know that he would very much like to have a chat with Victor in the afternoon, at the Embassy. Rama confirmed that it was totally possible and that was that.

The hours dragged on at Rover's office. He couldn't really focus on anything. The ambassador didn't seem at all interested in a failed drug bust or nightly experiments in the mountains. Of course, no mention was made of any spaceships. Some German intelaffs ("intelligence affiliates") had been in touch about the whereabouts of one Ilse Grokmann, last seen en route from Bangkok to the PSYNC village, but Rover simply refused to be the one who told them that she'd probably been integrated in a massive red light from outer space. Far better to remain silent.

Right on the appointed hour, there was a knock on Rover's door, and his secretary introduced Victor.

"Hello, again. You look well and rested", Rover said.

"It's probably the mountain air up there. Or maybe there's just something in the water?"

"Yes, who knows? Please, have a seat", Rover said and pulled out a chair.

On the table was a tape recorder, some glasses and a bottle of mineral water. Victor helped himself to a glass. Rover pressed the "record" button.

"Am I under arrest or something?", Victor asked.

"Let's just say you and I need to talk a bit. There's been too much going on and you simply pop up everywhere. I'm just curious, we could say."

"Alright. I'd be happy to answer your questions. I don't feel I have anything to hide. Not from you. Not from anyone."

"Well, that's a good start. First, is Mary your mother?"

"So they say."

"Who?"

"The people I grew up with. Up in the mountains."

"Who's your father? An American?"

Victor nodded and drank some water. Rover flipped through some papers and looked puzzled.

"You have a Nepalese passport. Why not an American? Do you know who your father is?"

"No idea on both questions. I guess I'm as much Nepalese as American as anything else."

"But it doesn't work that way. If you're American you're supposed to have an American passport. Why are you so vehemently against America?"

Victor laughed, and then drank some more water.

"Am I? Not at all. If I'm American, please provide me with an American passport. I'll accept it, I'll even treat it gently."

"So you're not anti-American?"

"On the contrary. I've been there many times and I love it."

"OK. Happy to hear that. Now, where did you get the acid? I know you had some up there..."

"I guess it's in my genes", Victor replied.

"Really? Then I have to ask you that you take them off right now."

"I mean, in my g-e-n-e-s. My mom is basically an old hippie, and so was my father according to what I've heard. Some of it must have spilled over."

"And, what, you tapped that into a bottle somehow?", Rover asked, looking as puzzled as he was.

"No! Are you out of your mind? Anyway, I understand you. The acid at the festival must have been brought by someone and poured into the drinks somehow. I have no idea. People drink, people smoke, people drop some acid. Who's to say what's right and wrong these days?"

"So you had nothing to do with that, then? But who did it?"

"Who indeed?", Victor said. "If you ask me, and you are, I think it smells of a covert government operation. A frame-op, an experiment. Those things have happened before. You know what I mean: the MKULTRA experiments was just the top of the iceberg, right? Everybody was sniffing around, trying things out. But we're not living in the 50s or 60s anymore, Rover. Come to think of it, I have never really lived in the 60s.

These things exist though. Most everyone I've talked to remains hush-hush about it for a very good reason, and that is something called emotional and factual discrepancy. You experience one thing and that one thing is great, a real life changer, but you're brainwashed into thinking it's not true or real. Or, even worse, that it's something wrong. I'm not saying any of it is right or wrong. Speaking of slightly wrong, how did you even know there was acid in the punch in the first place?"

“That’s probably classified information. Probably very classified. But seriously, what exactly are you after, Victor? Do you believe in reincarnation and all that mumbo-jumbo?”

“Well, I think carnations are very beautiful, that’s what I think. What I’m after? I’m after myself, and nothing and no one else. Listen, Rover, if I have lived a weird life and if I have had weird friends, do you think it’s appropriate that I should apologize for that?”

“No”, Rover answered after thinking a while.

“No, that’s right. And I won’t. Think about it. I’ve grown up being hailed, from day one, as someone special, in this beautiful country among beautiful people. They have believed in me, and some of them still do. Should I say no? Should I say yes? You tell me.”

“Tell you what?”, Rover asked.

“Tell me where the truth lies in all this, and I will tell you a story of a young boy who believed in magic, and who still believes in magic. It’s a pretty long story, so you’ll have to brace yourself.”

“Uh, that won’t be necessary. I have to ask you this, though: Have you ever been involved in any criminal activity?”

“I guess so”, Victor said, knowing this would wake Rover up a bit. It did.

“Really? What? You can tell me. Actually, you have to tell me.”

“Unconscious tax-evasion, incompetence, disregard for financial matters and life-long self-deceit.”

“Are you being a smart-ass?”

“Yes, I guess I am. I’m sorry. It’s just that I’m a bit perplexed. If you suspect me of something, it’s better if you ask straight out instead.”

“I don’t suspect anything, Victor. All we have is a whole lot of weirdness that doesn’t make sense. And you’re in the middle of it.”

“OK, then I’m guilty of a whole lot of weirdness that doesn’t make sense, and of being in the middle of it. But that isn’t really a crime yet, is it? I’m an artist, Rover, what would you expect? I think a good thing to start with is to ask yourself: ‘Cui Bono?’ Who gains? Who is afraid of me and why? What could I possibly do that could harm anyone or anything? I’m just an avant-garde reactionary who enjoys a bit of peace and quiet."

Rover laid his papers aside. He drank some water too, as the heat was making them both sweat.

"You know what?," Rover began. "I wouldn't say that your party was a bit of peace and quiet. Far from it. I believe you but at the same time I still don't believe in what you say. To me, you're an American. You have an American father, according to both yourself and your mother, who is an American citizen. What can I say? You're an American. Where the hell have you been?

Then we get these reports of heavy telepathic communications. That is something we're very interested in, by the way. How do you do it? Then we get all kinds of intel that you're some kind of magic guy, or that you're a Satanist, that you've actually been in touch with ETs, or that you're putting together an occult group to overthrow... I don't know what actually... And many other things on top of that. But you should be happy to hear I simply don't believe in it anymore. We don't believe in it. That's that. I think you're just a very confused guy who's been a victim of circumstance. Perhaps we can agree on that? And what happened the other night will of course stay between us, right? That has been agreed upon too, right?"

"Rover... If you yourself had all those rumors and then some buzzing around you, wouldn't you yourself be pretty confused?"

They both laughed. Victor looked Rover straight in the eye and didn't let go. Rover started feeling quite uneasy. What did Victor want? Rover could hear the flies in the small room. What should he say now?, he wondered. It was as if time and all sounds had suddenly stopped. He couldn't think of anything else to say or do.

"Silence is golden, right, Rover?", Victor said quietly. "I basically only have one final thing to say... I am that I am. Now, please be so kind as to get me my American passport."

53

Outside the American Embassy, an old black Mercedes waited. As Victor exited, Govinda Harrer stepped out of the car to greet him.

"Everything OK?", the old man asked.

"Spitzenklasse, Señor Harrer," Victor replied. "They even gave me a temporary American passport. Can you believe it?"

They laughed, got into the car and drove off. Rover watched them through a window, not certain how he would recount or report the interrogation. Underneath the surface there was a lot. He knew it and a few others around the world knew it too. They just didn't know what. Ritterstadt was a full time weirdo. But maybe that was it? Victor Ritterstadt was a danger to no one but possibly himself.

"I am that I am?" Rover recognized that from somewhere. While thinking about it, he took the cassette of their conversation and slowly pulled out all the magnetic tape. Then he proceeded to shred his files and papers on Victor Ritterstadt, containing reports from other agencies, notes on possible Ritterstadt coercion or employment, and a drawing Victor had made for him as they were about to part: a smiling bald man, obviously Ritterstadt himself, saying 'bye-bye' happily.

The documents dealing with the passport, including the extra passport photos of Victor (smiling even more) just taken at the Embassy, were filed and left with a secretary, together with a note saying "100 % 'lost' American. Please file as 'classified' and report to US HQ to integrate as citizen asap".

54

As the car moved through the landscape, Govinda Harrer started coughing. First discretely, then more aggressively.

"Are you OK?", Victor asked.

"I don't feel so good."

Victor could see Govinda was sweating more than usual.

"Do you want me to drive?", he asked.

"No, we're almost there."

As they parked the car in the village, Govinda was coughing violently and also started shaking. Victor rushed out and called for help. Rama came running, as did some of the students.

"Call a doctor!", Victor shouted.

"No doctor...", Govinda coughed.

They carried him into his house and put him to bed. Rama asked everyone to leave, including Victor.

Mary, who'd heard the shouting, joined Victor and the others outside Govinda's house.

"What's going on?", she asked.

"It's Govinda... He just started coughing and gasping for air. It was horrible."

"Don't worry, he'll be fine...", she said. "He's so strong."

They waited anxiously. Mary had never seen Victor look afraid or even hesitant. She held his hand. He was in cold sweats too.

Rama called for Victor, who rushed in.

"What?", he asked.

"It's like this, Victor... He's going now... He wants to see you... Go..."

Victor entered the room. Strong, reliable Govinda Harrer was coughing and shaking in bed. Victor sat down by the bed and took his hand.

"Govinda, Govinda...", he said silently. "Don't leave us now."

"Victor...", Govinda whispered. "I don't want to... But I have to..."

"What's going on...?", Victor continued.

"I've been ill for some time..."

More coughing. Then Harrer seemed to calm down. His body relaxed.

"Govinda..."

"Listen... What I have you can have... Show the photos to your mother..."

"Yes... Yes, I'll do that..."

"Tell her I loved her... Victor... I'm your father..."

"I know that", Victor said and started crying. "I know it. I have known it a long time. Thank you for everything. I love you very much, Govinda. Do you want to see her?"

"I can't... Just tell her..."

Victor felt Govinda's grip of his hand tightening. He closed his eyes. The old man tried mumbling "Om mane padme hum" but couldn't keep it up. Victor helped him by saying it over and over. "Om mane padme hum... Om mane padme hum... Om mane padme hum...", in between tears and sobbing. Then the gripping hand suddenly let go and Govinda's body lay still, lifeless and finally at peace. Victor cried violently and held on to Govinda's hand.

After a while Rama entered and they hugged each other and cried. Mary and the others who had been outside came in too. They looked at Govinda's body, once so full of life and now empty as a shell on a beach. No one said anything but just looked and hugged and cried. There was absolutely nothing to say.

When everyone found out, the people of the village started bringing flowers and lighting candles and incense. Everyone came inside slowly and silently to pay their final respects. Also to Victor, who was heartbroken and just couldn't stop sobbing.

55

They stayed up all night to reminisce and take care of each other. Some were sleeping for a few hours and then waking up again. Victor couldn't. He sat by the corpse, together with Mary.

"Just before he went, he said he loved you", Victor said.

"Well, I loved him too", Mary replied.

"No, I mean really loved you. Do you know who he was? Can you understand now?"

"What do you mean?", Mary asked him.

"I know that you were completely zonked back then, and that's fine. Who knows what you were up to? But you should know that Govinda Harrer was my father."

Mary looked at him. Was this some kind of bad joke? No, the time wasn't really right, not even for Victor's peculiar sense of humor. Could it be? She couldn't remember, no matter how hard she tried. But it was obvious from the film that he had been at that same party in 1970. He had come with Big Baba to pick her up at the hotel. Then he was gone. But he had been there for Victor all through his childhood, teaching him what he knew.

"Did you know all along?", she asked.

"It was more like a feeling", Victor said. "I mean, we almost looked alike. I'll show you some photos later. He used to look like I do now. Also, he once told me I couldn't do something. I can't even remember what it was. But it struck me that he had forcefully said no to me. No one else ever did. Maybe they didn't dare to. But he did. I think I realized it back then. Anyway, now he told me."

"Didn't he have any family?", Mary asked.

"I have no idea. Sometimes he was away doing his projects. Taking pictures, writing, and later on the lightshows. He went to Switzerland some times. He was from Switzerland."

On Govinda's desk lay his Swiss passport.

"Born on April 16th, 1943", Victor read. "That means we had our party on his birthday. Why didn't he tell us, I wonder? He was an odd one, that's for sure."

"It was a beautiful birthday party then, secret or not. He seemed very happy. And what a piece of art he created for us."

56

In the morning, they knew they had to deal with Govinda's body, and also report his death to the Swiss Embassy. They did. It was decided that the body would be cremated after examination. An ambulance arrived some hours later and picked up the physical remains of Govinda Harrer.

"How are you feeling?", Mary asked Victor as the car drove away.

"OK. There is something so final, so inevitable in death. It sounds strange, but to be close to it can be a necessary reminder of certain things. Not to take life for granted. How are you?"

"OK too. If what you say is true I was probably more out of my mind than I can remember. Or perhaps dare to remember. Do you think I may have created my own memories out of desires?"

"Certainly. In fact, that's what most people do. If you're up for it, I think we should go through his stuff. You know, the photos and things."

"Sure", Mary said, a little bit afraid of what they would find.

Candles were still burning in his little cottage. Pictures of Govinda were present, aglow in the light from the candles and incense sticks.

"Where to begin?", Victor asked.

Govinda had a lot of material in his little cottage. Books, mainly on mountaineering and Buddhism, made his bookshelves sway under pressure. In a cupboard they didn't find clothes but several large boxes, containing cameras, negatives and photographic prints. Majestic Asian landscapes, portraits, animals, plants, mountains, all in vast amounts. He had been all over many times, it seemed. Soon they found some cartons saying "Kathmandu 1969-1971". It was packed with prints, still in good shape and seemingly untainted by time.

Flipping through images of Freak Street, hippies, parties, Babas and Buddhist monks at Bodhnath, they eventually found what they were looking for. There were several portraits of Mary that were apparently taken in a one-to-one setting. Even some taken in a mirror, showing Mary and Govinda together. And then of Victor as an infant, post-Mary.

They both cried as they saw these photos. Mary was in a state of slight shock.

"This is so incredible...", she gasped.

"Life often is", Victor replied and looked at the photos over and over again. He had never seen them before and he wondered why Govinda hadn't showed them at all.

"Have I been living in a total illusion?", Mary whispered.

"I would perhaps not call it total", Victor said. "I do think you had a wonderful time and that everything was highly real to you. 'Highly' as in 'High'. But I also think you burnt out on the acid. Mosely-Manly was a skilled alchemist and it was potent gold he manufactured. To be on that for longer than one trip will certainly do things to your mind. I believe you lost it there for a while, got very, very scared and then painted a pretty picture of a more trivial, debauched groupie-trip. Then your own construct of a bad conscience took over and made you leave your own little love child on the other side of the planet."

"But I did have sex with the Fateful Head!", Mary said.

"I'm sure you did, mom. Well, maybe you did. But there was also someone there you deliberately chose to forget altogether. I really wonder why."

"I wish I knew", Mary said. "I really do. This is just one huge mystery. And it hurts."

Mary again looked at the photo of her and Govinda together.

This would have to sink in, she thought. Deep, deep. She realized though, that the grip of her old vague anxieties, the ones that had been in her mental luggage on returning to Nepal, were dissolving in the midst of this new (or, rather, old) mystery.

"Yes, mom, that's right. Without mystery there can be no accurate description of the truth", Victor said and left her with the photos.

At dinner that night they talked about what to do next. Everyone was sad and the atmosphere muted.

"I just got a call from the Swiss Embassy", Rama said. "He had no relatives that they could see. There's a house in Zürich that he owned and also a house in the Alps. I think it's good if you have a look at this, Victor. He left it in our safe about a year ago."

He handed Victor an envelope. Hesitantly, Victor opened it and read to the others.

"In the case of my death, I leave all of my worldly possessions to Victor Ritterstadt, my biological son, c/o the Patanjali Neophile Yoga Retreat Center in Nepal. As I don't know exactly where he is as I write this, I leave it to Rama, the Center's administrator, to settle this, so that Victor can get access to what's rightfully his. I hope and trust that the Swiss authorities will be helpful in seeing to that everything will be handled in a correct manner. Signed, Ernst Albert Harrer."

Everyone was silent. Victor folded the paper and put it back into the envelope.

"Thanks and praise to you, dad", he said after wiping some tears out of his eyes.

"What are we going to do with his ashes?", Rama asked.

"We're going to smuggle him into Tibet, back to Kailash", Victor suggested. "Or at least up into the hills here. He'll be happy as long as there are mountains around him. Or maybe we could build a shrine right here?"

Everyone agreed this would be a wonderful thing, and then finished their meals in silence.

57

One week after Harrer's demise, the ashes were sent up in an urn. A ceremony had been prepared and all the people in the village were present. Close to Harrer's cottage, they had cleared a space next to some rocks. A big hole had been dug, around which everyone had assembled. There were friends from Kathmandu present that Rama didn't know personally, including an elderly gentleman from the Swiss Embassy.

"It's a beautiful day today", Victor began. "It would have been even more beautiful had you still been with us, Govinda. But now you're not and there's nothing we can do about it. That's life – a juggling of definites-so-called, quite often far beyond our petty control. One definite though, was that you enriched our lives by your presence. Everyone, I'm sure, has their own Govinda story. I was taught so many things by you. Some by demonstration and words, but more often through silence and your setting good examples. True, you weren't always here. You were often away concocting your own magic through art and light. And when you gradually became more and more present, I was the one who disappeared out into the world, carrying with me the things that you had taught me – as well as other wisdoms from other people, of course.

I've got the energy you see
The awareness is here for one and all
The result is yet to come
Just don't lust for it
If we move by ourselves
Then it will too

Cast the seed into the field of night
And join us soon again
Work in a web of steeped horsehair
Indulge in the things we find there

We all love you for what you did
And surely what you still do
A box of brightness and you opened the lid
For me to see I'm here too

The key to it all

Would then be you
Like a flower in spring
It all comes true

When ecstasy comes over me
The strangest thing that has to be
Love is the law, love under will
Life begins when time stands still

I'd like to return to that magical silence of yours now. We can hear the breeze, the birds, the song of the mountains. That's quite enough, I think. Thanks, Ernst Albert. Thanks, Govinda. Thanks, Dad. Have a safe trip. Thanks."

Together with Rama, Victor poured out the ashes into the hole in the ground. Then he brought out the vials of LSD and poured what remained of it onto the ashes. Then they filled it with some earth and then a young, sturdy Rhododendron plant. After that, more earth around the plant, so it stood solidly, greeting the sun and accepting the praise of the people, who all poured a glass of water each over it. So it was done.

58

At a solemn reception after the funeral, most of the people assembled stayed on. The man from Switzerland introduced himself as Helmut Sander, shook Victor's hand and thanked him.

"It was very beautiful. He would have liked it. So you're actually his son? I can see it now that I know it. Let's take a walk."

They strolled off from the others.

"I just basically found out", Victor began. "He told me before he died. I've suspected it a long time though. Are you from the Embassy?"

"Yes, we could say that. And your mother never told you?"

"We just met basically. She thinks she was made pregnant by a psychedelic rock group."

"Ah, women!", Sander said. "Yes, I know that story. He even told it himself at times. At first I thought it was the truth. Those were crazy times here, I guess."

"Sure", Victor continued. "But if he was so certain all along, why didn't he tell us, tell me, tell my mother?"

"Have you noticed how history keeps repeating itself, Victor? I think your mother was a little bit, how should I put it, frail. When he talked about her, I could feel there was something there. But he was a sad, sad man."

"Really? I never really noticed that. I mean, when growing up here."

"I probably can't shock you any more than you've already been lately. But I want you to know a little bit about him. Are you up for that?"

"Absolutely", Victor replied.

"What I'm about to tell you will have to stay between us, and I hope you respect that. There are many people who think that you're simply an idiot with an immense ego. But I don't. I see you only as his son now, and I had and still have a deep respect for the man.

I assume you know nothing about his background. I do, because we researched it together. You know he was born in Switzerland in '43, and that's correct enough. His mother came there from a clinic in Norway."

"But I thought his mother was German?", Victor asked.

"Indeed she was. She was part of the SS Lebensborn experiment. You know, young solid German girls mated with SS men, and were then sent off to clinics to have the babies, who were then either taken care of or adopted by SS families. She was afraid that she'd never return to Germany and that she'd lose her child because of the war, so she ran away. Eventually she came to Switzerland and gave birth to baby Harrer. The entire experience, and the news after the war of what the SS had been up to upset her a great deal. She had to spend some time in a sanatorium for a while. That's a nicer word for mental hospital."

"This is a little bit much even for me", Victor whispered and stopped walking. The Swiss gentleman looked at him.

"I asked if you wanted to hear and you said yes. Anyway, things turned out well, didn't they? They led a good life in Switzerland, Harrer grew up, wanted to see the world, studied, just a normal life, you know. He didn't really know about the Lebensborn history until a secret group of Germans told him. They weren't out to harass him though, although many of these kids were harassed. They were out to recruit him into that group. I know, because I was in it myself."

"You're some kind of Nazi?", Victor asked.

"No, I'm not. Far from it. I was a frustrated youth, myself a Lebensborn child. There were older men who spurred us on, 'die Alte Kameraden', you know, die-hard old school types who never wanted to realize that the war, and everything else, was lost. Anyway, we became friends, although Harrer didn't want anything to do with that group. He made me question a lot of what was going on. We kept in touch. As I married and started a family, I wanted nothing more to do with it. So I quit. In many ways, Harrer helped me. He wrote me from Asia, saying it's so beautiful, and he suggested we come over. We met here in 1966, and me and my family haven't really left Nepal since then."

"What a story...", Victor said.

"Indeed. Perhaps you can even write that story some time. Please just wait until after I'm dead too. Now, can you see a psychological pattern that fits? A young man growing up with an absent father and a frail mother doubting her own sanity and traumatized by the conception, childbearing and birth? How this leads to children who desire to escape by traveling both in inner and outer worlds?"

"You're saying I'm stuck in a loop?", Victor asked and looked at the group of people, including Mary, who stood and talked calmly by Govinda's shrine.

"I'm not a psychologist, Victor", Sander answered. "I'm just saying that sometimes one needs to break the chain, to change the pattern. Harrer didn't do that: he became his own father in that sense, and your mother, just like his, was lost, as people today so eloquently put it, in space. Things have a tendency to repeat themselves, wouldn't you agree?"

"I hear you", Victor answered as they started walking again.

"Or perhaps it was only a cover-up to protect you, Victor."

"Protect me from what?"

"You're a charismatic fellow, I'll give you that. A little bit crazy perhaps, but charismatic. If those old Alte Kameraden, who are now probably young Alte Kameraden, knew that one of the Lebensborn kids in his turn has a charismatic, a little bit crazy son, perhaps they are willing to offer you something for something? A little bit of political limelight? Perhaps Harrer had foresight and didn't want it to be known? These people wouldn't touch someone from the loins of the Fateful Head, of course."

"I guess not", Victor said. "And that's probably as it should be. I appreciate your telling me these things."

"Don't mention it. Harrer was a good friend. Have you gone through his papers yet, by the way?"

"Not really. There's quite a lot. Why?"

"If there's anything I can do to help, just let me know. I'm good with papers and sorting things. I'm sure he has some interesting stuff I might be able to help you with. Let me know. Do you understand what I might be talking about?"

"Actually, I think I do", Victor replied. "Are you perhaps referring to a project that has to do with energy? Bicycles?"

Sander nodded. They walked further away from the others. When turning around and looking at the assembled crowd by Harrer's rhododendron plant, Sander lay his hand on Victor's shoulder.

"Yes, that's the one. Is it safe?", Sander asked.

"Well, yes, in the sense that no one's taken it away from me."

"Alright. You know where to contact me? All I want to say is that I can easily help finding financing for the project. In fact, I've been preparing for that for many years now. You should know that those plans are virgin territory. No one has patented anything from those plans and designs. You need to secure the idea on all levels. Please get in touch with me if you need assistance. Your father was actively involved in experimenting with certain of the techniques and let me tell you, there are a lot of people interested in this. Not all of them are as altruistic and friendly as he was."

"I see. So he or you or someone pushed everything on to me? Not that it matters. It seems to be a great thing. Overwhelming. I'll be in touch about it, don't worry. I just feel I need to get my head on straight again. Do some writing, traveling, you know, get back on track."

"You might want to consider focusing on this project too", Sander continued. "It has far reaching consequences, as I'm sure you can understand. No matter what, keep in touch. I'll write down all my numbers. Do you have a pen?"

Victor unbuttoned his shirt pocket and handed Sander the green mother of pearl fountain pen. Sander looked at it and then at Victor. He smiled.

"Very happy to see that you have this pen", Sander said.

"Why so?"

"EH is Ernst Harrer. It was your father's pen. I remember he thought it was lost. Did you by any chance get it when you were in the Balkan region?", Sander asked.

"That's right. From the same guy who pointed me to the plans and designs..."

"A friend", Sander said and smiled.

"A friend... Come to think about it, probably of the same generation as you and my father", Victor said.

"Perhaps. Well, anyway, here you go, here are all the numbers you need. And your pen. Take care of it. It will bring you good luck. A good pen always finds its rightful owner. This one certainly has."

They shook hands and said good-bye. Sander waved to his driver, who started the car, pulled up and opened the door. Victor watched the car drive down the small and winding road, followed by a trail of dry dust.

"I hope and pray there will be no more radical and mind altering experiences and information for a while", he thought to himself while walking back to the crowd. "At least not until tomorrow."

59

Over the coming days, Victor talked to Rama about the energy project. Rama, being an open-minded fellow, didn't overreact enthusiastically but just patiently listened to Victor's ideas and need of feedback. Mary was brought in on it too, which was a good thing. Having worked with patents and registrations almost all of her adult life, she provided the needed bits to secure all the relevant details of the design and function. They agreed that when all of that was safely taken care of, they'd bring in Sander and try to make some kind of business plan. The idea was to have the Yoga center profit from the project, now tentatively called "Cyclife Grade A". They formulated every last little detail and Mary decided to go back to New York and register everything there, as she knew all the patent routines and the right people to speed up the process.

Victor had decided to go back to Berlin, end his little base camp there, then go to Zürich to settle his inheritance from Harrer and then possibly go back to Macedonia to see what Veronica was up to. He was a little bit stressed by it all but realized that all of these gifts couldn't just be ignored. Eventually, he'd have the time to sit down in peace and quiet and write some new stories, but first the real life ones would have to be handled in a mature manner.

60

Victor also met with Sander again and talked about project details. It was agreed that the safest option would be to set up a Swiss company that actually owned the patent for the Cyclife-constructions, with Victor as beneficiary. He could then hand over as much money to any Yoga village as he wanted. Sander could set up the company in time for Victor's arrival in Zürich and even offered to meet him there to help.

"I hope you understand that I'm a little bit overwhelmed", Victor told him. "Why are you doing this?"

"It's life, Victor. You have been leading a life of the mind and the mind only. To a great extent, Harrer was just like that also. But your mind is always a part of a greater reality or a greater mind. In this wider mind things also affect the real, tangible world. I would probably call it causal reality. You know, cause and effect. The thing is, your ideals and your preferences are also mirrored in this causal sphere. I guess this is where the real magic lies, in this intersection. Anyway, that's what your father said. That, on the whole, it's pretty pointless to be on a mind trip if it never coincides or has the chance to leave traces and trails for others."

"You mean like in art and literature?", Victor asked.

"Sure, but that's just one fragment of the totality of possibilities. Our little project is another facet of this. One that has to do with science and energy and money and a change of destinies… I mean, on a really large scale…”

“This really sounds far out. I never expected to hear this from you, Sander.”

“Don’t forget that my mind is a conglomerate that touches upon yours and is related to yours. We have a very special background, one that stems from the other, darker side of the rainbow-colored mirror. My father was an SS officer, as was your grandfather. Tesla’s plans for the energy transmission was stolen by the SS in Belgrade at some point during the war. I’ll spare you the details how me and Harrer later on found them. But we did. The important thing is that Tesla’s ideas are put to use. It’s a way of correcting or balancing history a bit. If I can be helpful in that process, it makes me feel good.”

“I hear you. I’ve ceased to be surprised about all these weird things. But I agree, let’s try and make the most of it. So I’ll see you in Zürich then?”

“Indeed. Stay in touch and I’ll make the arrangements for the company and so on. Everything needs to be solid as rock. Solid as the Himalayas.”

“And as the Swiss Alps too”, Victor laughed.

They finished their coffee in Sander’s lush and peaceful bungalow garden. The birds were singing a song of hope and wonder in the midst of the distant, muted roar of the Kathmandu traffic.

61

Mary sat on her bed and brought out her old journal. She’d brought it back to Nepal, as she knew that it would at some point be time to start working on it again. Now, that time had come.

“I feel I need to look at things from another perspective, not my own.” That was the very last thing she had written in her book, before going to the resting home in America early in 1972. She took her pen and slowly (but not hesitantly) wrote right after that sentence: “I feel I need to look at things from another perspective, this time completely my own.” She smiled.

There was a knock on her door. She lay the notebook aside and opened. It was Victor, who wanted to go for a walk with her. They strolled over to the road and walked up the hill. After a while, they stopped and looked down over the valley and the village, so peaceful and still in the lush landscape.

"Sure, I'll do this thing now with the patents, but I want to come back here as soon as possible", Mary told Victor. "I actually think I want to stay here forever."

"That sounds great. Rama will be here waiting for you, of course. And you'll be busy enough with the project, I'm sure."

"How about you? Will you be here again after Switzerland?"

"At some point, sure, but not just now. We have to focus on this thing now. For good or bad, it will change a lot. I just hope it'll be for the better", Victor said.

"What do you mean? Of course it'll be for the better if we can save energy and all contribute to the energy we consume..."

"Sure, that's all fine and dandy. What I mean is how much this will demand of me. I mean, time wise. I feel I have other things to do. In that sense, I really do need your help here. And Rama's. And Sander's. If you can deal with it, I'd be overjoyed. Then if we can save some energy and make some money for the Yoga center, that'd be great too. I'm just afraid it'll be a little bit too big a project."

"Time will tell", Mary replied. "You've been blessed by your own freedom, I understand that. And I think you're afraid of losing it. Am I right?"

"Maybe. But I feel happy about it too. Complacency is a killer. One needs to be shook up once in a while. But that doesn't mean I should let my own will be subdued by this kind of general altruism. That would be bad, I think. Unnatural."

"I think you need to learn how to merge the two. I can't see any discrepancy at all."

"You're probably right. I'm probably a little bit shook up by these past developments. I need to get away to clear my mind. I can only do that by writing. I know myself that well. It's the only thing that really works. That's just the way it is."

"But what happens if Lucy's pregnant? Will you come back then?", Mary asked.

"Maybe, maybe not. I think you can handle that one, mom. Make amends, take care of it, pay penance, call it what you want. Try and reincarnate Govinda into the baby. I just want to do what I want do. And that's all there's to it."

"So what exactly do you want to do?", Mary asked him.

"Well, someone said that the library is endless. Volumes upon volumes filled with deception, not forgetting self deceit. Me, I'm happy to be a writer, an artist with a lucid mind. But am I really? I am just a mirror, reflecting your own image. If I appear sad, whose fault is that? The library is essentially filled with hopeless mirrors, desperately reflecting each other and eventually cracking. I mean, if life is so great, then why isn't it?

That said, I want to do what I suspect every writer wants to do: live and work in New York, get some Hollywood business, and make lots of money. It may not be cosmic on the grand scale of things, but it really is what I want. Now that I am an American citizen of sorts, I'd be stupid not to make use of that, right?"

"What about love and happiness and inner peace? And the possibility of fatherhood?"

"Oh, I never really thought about that. It sounds good. I'm not opposed to it. And yes, I'll keep coming back here to do lectures and keep everyone happy. I care about this place. It is my home in so many ways. But at the same time I just want to write, preferably in New York, and then get some Hollywood business, and make lots of money."

"OK. So why don't you?"

"Well, who says I'm not?"

"I am. Because you're right here in the Himalayas with me, your own mother."

"Am I really? I wouldn't be so sure of that. If I were you, that is. But then I'm not, now, am I?"

www.ingramcontent.com/pod-product-compliance
Ingram Content Group UK Ltd.
Pitfield, Milton Keynes, MK11 3LW, UK
UKHW040009200726
13854UKWH00001B/113

9 789198 624212